CW01643191

MURDER IN CRIMSON VELVET

A BRIDAL SHOP COZY MYSTERY

KAREN SUE WALKER

This is a work of fiction. All names, characters, locales, and incidents are products of the author's imagination and any resemblance to actual people, places, or events is coincidental.

To learn more about the author and her books, visit www.karensuewalker.com. While you're there, sign up and get a free story!

To Kalena

A promise is a promise.

Your creativity and imagination inspire me every day.
I'm grateful to have you in my life.

CHAPTER 1

In the twenty-seven years that Max Walters had been on the earth, she had never been good at waiting. Not at the age of six years old opening the presents under the tree two days before Christmas, and not now.

She paced among displays of exotic flowers in galvanized baskets that lined the flower shop owned by her good friend Eric Mancini. Normally, she felt at peace in his shop, with its white oak floors and beautiful hand-painted murals of flower gardens. She noticed a new quote painted artfully on the wall. *Love is a flower. You've got to let it grow.*

She took a deep breath, inhaling the intoxicating scent of the blooms surrounding her and stared at the back of the room where Eric had slipped away after barely a single word. Was something wrong? He wouldn't tell her on the phone why he wanted to talk to her when he called last night. Why was he being so mysterious?

He emerged from the back room with two mugs of coffee, which he placed on the cafe table in the middle of the shop. He pulled out a chair for Max. Apparently, this would be a sit-down kind of conversation.

"I have a proposition for you, Max," he said, pausing dramatically.

"Yes?" Now her curiosity was definitely piqued.

His smile told her he enjoyed making her wait. It also said no one was dying, so she smiled back, and her breathing returned to normal. He sat down across from her, took a sip of his coffee, and leaned back in his chair. "How would you like to open your own bridal salon?"

Max didn't know what to say. It wasn't that she hadn't thought about opening her own shop, but she figured it would be years from now when she was older and more financially secure. She'd worked at Wedding Belles Bridal Shop off and on since her teens, so she knew she had the experience.

"Aren't you going to say anything?" Eric asked, looking a little disappointed at her lack of reaction.

"I'd like to have my own shop someday," she admitted, not sure what she thought about his suggestion. "Why are you asking?"

"Sweetie, you've talked about wanting to start your own business. Why not now? I have investments that are doing fine but putting my money in stocks and bonds is no fun at all. I thought about opening another flower shop, but it would be a lot of work. Investing in a bridal salon would be a new adventure, and we'd get to work together, too, which is an added bonus."

"Right." Max crossed her arms and studied him. "Okay, let's hear it. What's the real reason?" Max stared him down, waiting for him to fess up.

"Fine. I'm bored." He leaned back in his chair. "I remember how happy I felt when I started up my shop. It was so exciting looking for a space to rent and working with the interior designers and learning everything I needed to know about running my own business. I've thought about getting a hobby. I even agreed to let Jonathan teach me how to golf."

"You must be in love if you let him talk you into golfing."

"Let's just say things are going well. But I need more in my life than my shop and my boyfriend. I need a new challenge."

"And I'm your challenge?" Max's eyebrows rose in mock indignation.

"Honey, you're always a challenge," Eric said teasingly.

"Hey!" she objected. She considered herself to be pretty low maintenance, at least most of the time.

"I'm just kidding." He leaned forward, reaching across the table to take her hand. "You're my best friend, and I want you to be happy. We both know you're not going to be content to work for Darlene forever. I don't want you to move back to New York and force me to find a new best friend."

"You wouldn't!" Now her indignation was authentic.

"Of course, I wouldn't. But I'd rather have you here.

Besides, you need to spread your wings. But, you know, without actually going anywhere."

"But where would I even open a bridal salon? Crystal Shores isn't big enough for two."

"I thought about that. You could open one in Newport Beach. They have one of those big chain bridal stores, but they don't have any boutique shops. I think your salon would be a big hit there. And wouldn't it be fun to be partners?"

"Partners?" Max asked, wondering what she might be getting herself into. Eric had been one of her best friends ever since he'd done her parents a favor and taken her to the prom when she didn't have a date. They were able to talk to each other about anything and everything. She'd told Eric stuff she hadn't told anyone else. Would being business partners put a strain on their friendship?

"I would be a minority partner, of course. You'd make all the final decisions, but maybe I can help with the business side of things. And the decorating, of course!" He did love decorating and had exquisite taste. He had completely redecorated his shop when he decided French Provincial was too common, and now it had a more modern, upscale look that was even lovelier. "Also, I already have an excellent lawyer and a business manager, but you'll need to get your own lawyer to go over the contract before you sign it."

"Wow. You've given it a lot of thought." This was already getting complicated. "I don't know. Working at Wedding Belles is the only job I've ever had besides being a pattern maker in New York. What if the shop doesn't do well, and I lose all the money you've invested?"

"Listen to me. I was lucky enough to have someone believe in me so I could open my flower shop."

She laughed. "You invested your own money that you inherited from your grandfather."

"That's right. I believed in me. And look how well it worked out. I believe in you, Max. I can afford to lose my investment, but I know I won't. I don't think you even realize how talented you are. And you already have a following. You'll be busy from the day you open."

"I need to think this over," Max said. "It's a really big decision." Boy, was it ever.

"Of course. I want you to think it over. But in the meantime, I found a shop that is available near Fashion Island that I think is perfect, so I called my real estate agent to arrange for us to see it. Would you just humor me and go check it out?"

Max knew Eric didn't like to take no for an answer, but this was her decision to make. And if she wasn't ready, then he'd have to just accept that. Still, what could it hurt to take a look at a shop space? It might be fun.

"My own bridal shop," she murmured. She felt a grin take over her face. She liked the sound of that.

~

MAX NEEDED TO GO TO HER THINKING PLACE: THE beach. A short walk later and she felt her toes sinking into the cool sand. The grey skies of June's gloom didn't dampen her mood. The fact that Eric believed in her meant the world to her.

Turning down the job as an assistant designer in New York when her previous employer offered it to her last March had been a difficult decision, but she loved her life in Crystal Shores with her father and friends. Maybe she was in a rut with her job as bridal consultant, seamstress, and sometime wedding gown designer, but running her own shop was a big step. She felt excited thinking about it, but was she ready? Would it be better to wait until she could do it on her own? What would it be like being business partners with Eric? He had a strong personality, and she wasn't sure he'd let her make her own decisions. Still, she would certainly have more control than she did now, working for Darlene Chandler. She could order the wedding dresses she wanted to stock and design gowns without her interference. Her boss had to have the final say in everything, which could be very frustrating.

More importantly, she didn't want to put a strain on her friendship with Eric, since friends and family meant more to her than anything else. She'd realized that a few months ago when she'd turned down the New York job to stay in Crystal Shores.

The only thing lacking was her love life. She'd been in love with Andy Fuller since she was a teenager, and it wasn't until he married someone else that she realized it was never meant to be. She'd gone out on a few dates since then, but she decided she would be patient and wait for the right guy to show up in her life. Unless it took too long, and then she'd rethink her plan.

Crystal Shores was her home, and although Eric worried she might move back to New York, she knew she was staying, surrounded by people she cared about. And the beach just a short walk away! She came to the beach almost every morning to clear her head and start her day with a peaceful mind. In the silence between the waves, she heard the barks of the sea lions and the ka-ka-ka of the seagulls. Her worries seemed insignificant when she stared out at the miles of ocean that stretched out before her. A sandpiper darted about, poking its nose in the sand.

Max weighed the pros and cons of opening her own shop in her mind but realized it would take more than one walk on the beach to be able to come to a decision. Besides, she had a job to get to. She brushed off the sand that stubbornly clung to her feet, put her sandals back on, and walked the short distance to her apartment over her dad's garage. After a quick shower, she slipped into a royal blue knit dress that fell just above her knees and wrapped a colorful scarf around her neck. She looked through her cupboards for something to eat. These past few days, she'd missed her morning breakfasts with her dad. She smiled, knowing he'd be back from his trip later today and tomorrow morning they'd be having coffee and oatmeal together.

She found a protein drink in the back of her refrigerator left over from when she had decided to lose weight last month. She'd since decided that she looked fine just the way she was, average. Not model-thin like so many women in this town, but they spent hours in the gym to look that way or resorted to liposuction. She wasn't interested in either.

After downing the protein drink, she ran the hot iron through her shoulder length brown hair to take out the frizz from her morning walk. As she did every workday, she carefully applied mascara, eye shadow and lipstick. Her boss Darlene often reminded her how much appearances mattered, though Max had her own ideas on the subject. Wasn't it what was inside that mattered? She headed down the stairs, walking the four blocks to Coast Highway. The street they lived on, Rose Street, had escaped the redevelopment that overran Crystal Shores, turning it into a town of mini mansions. She passed pastel cottages with impressive displays of early summer blooms, stopping several times to smell fragrant roses. It was like aromatherapy on the go.

She turned the corner onto Coast Highway and saw the sign for the Wedding Belles Bridal Shop. What would Darlene say about her opening her own shop? She'd worry about that later.

CHAPTER 2

Max stuck her head into the office to say good morning to Darlene who sat peering at the computer with her glasses low on her nose. Darlene's jet-black hair, pulled up into a sensible bun, gave her the look of a portly ballet teacher, and she wore her signature bright red lipstick. Max tried to push the idea of her own bridal shop out of her mind, went into the workroom, and got to work installing grommets on a leather corset. She ignored the ringing phone, knowing Darlene would pick it up. She stayed focused on her task until she heard the front door jingle. She recognized the voice of Darlene's husband Kenneth.

"Anastasia's in labor!" Max heard him say.

"Max, come here please," Darlene called out, and Max went into the showroom.

"Hello, Kenneth," she said. "How are you?"

"I'm in a panic," he answered. "Our costumer swore she wasn't due to have her baby for weeks, and now she'd gone into labor. It's less than a week until dress rehearsal and half the costumes for *Romeo and Juliet* aren't finished."

Anastasia Vanderweele was the costumer at the theater Kenneth ran. She was quite good at her job, but often ran behind and needed help at the last minute.

"Don't worry, dear," Darlene cooed at her husband. "We'll help out, won't we Max?"

Max was pretty sure that by 'we' Darlene meant Max. It wasn't the first time she'd been asked to help, but it had always been for just a day or two to finish up a few hems before a show opened. Darlene called on her to do every sort of task at Wedding Belles Bridal but doing double duty at the theater seemed to be above and beyond the call of duty.

"I'll pay you, of course," Kenneth said. "The same rate you earn here."

"Fine," Max said. There went her nice, quiet week. "I'll get my things together."

"Thank you, Max," Kenneth said, sounding relieved. "And thank you, darling," he said to his wife. "I don't know what I'd do without you."

"Don't worry, dear," Darlene said in her sweetest voice. "You'll never have to find out."

Max went back to the workroom and grabbed her sewing kit and sweater. When she returned to the workroom, she asked, "Can I get a ride?"

"I was hoping to have a talk with my wife," Kenneth said. "I was planning to take her to lunch if I can convince her to tear herself away from her work."

The theater was about a mile south, one block off

Coast Highway, and Max wanted to get to the theater as soon as possible to see how much needed to be done. She lived so close to work, she hadn't bothered to buy a car when she moved back from New York last year. She'd got along fine without one so far.

"Why don't you walk? It's not that far," Darlene said. "And it's a lovely day."

Max answered with a sigh and looked down at her high-heeled sandals. If she'd planned on walking, she would have worn different shoes.

"Maybe if you didn't wear those ridiculous sandals," Darlene said, "it wouldn't be a problem. I always told you to be more practical. When I was in the workforce, sandals like those were completely unacceptable, and no woman would go to work without wearing stockings."

Max had heard this lecture before. She was about to point out that things had changed but decided not to bother. It seemed that all of Darlene's sweetness was used up on Kenneth.

The jingling of the door announced an arrival. Keiko, their assistant, entered wearing a white shirt with a Peter Pan collar, a full pink skirt with petticoat, and pink platform Mary Jane shoes. She'd pulled her dark brown hair up into two pigtails.

"Keiko can take you," Darlene announced.

Keiko stopped in her tracks and looked at the two women, her boss and her mentor. "Okey-dokey," she said, and turned around to walk back out the door.

Max followed her outside, Keiko's platform shoes clunking on the sidewalk. She stopped for a moment to let her eyes adjust to the bright mid-morning sun that had broken through the clouds. The cool, ocean breeze made her smile thinking about how hot it must be in New York right now.

Keiko already had the car started by the time she got in. She turned to Max and asked, "Where am I taking you?"

Max explained the crisis she was on her way to avert at the Crystal Shores Playhouse where *Romeo and Juliet* would be opening in less than a week.

"How exciting. I want to help. May I come over after work?"

Keiko's enthusiasm was infectious, and Max cheered up about the idea of helping with the costumes. "Of course. I'll see how much still needs to get done. Maybe I can get Kenneth to pay both of us."

"I would like to work at a theater. Is it very different working on costumes rather than wedding gowns?"

"Completely different. Every stitch has to be perfect on a wedding gown. Costumes are sewn as quickly as possible, and as long as they look good from the audience, no one cares what they look like up close."

"I wish I could come with you now. When you hired me, you did not mention how demanding Darlene could be," Keiko said.

"I remember you told me she would love you. And she does." The truth was, everyone loved Keiko. She was half Japanese, raised in southern California, and had rarely seen her father who had returned to Japan when she was a small child.

"She has an interesting way of showing it. Sometimes she reminds me of Yubaba in *Spirited Away*. She's the witch who runs the bathhouse."

"Are you calling Darlene a witch?" Max said, teasing. Max had become used to her referencing all her favorite movies. When Keiko got to college, she changed her name from Cathy to Keiko and embraced Japanese culture, including Anime.

Keiko looked chagrined. "No. She's just always barking orders at me."

"Darlene's not big on the positive reinforcement, but she appreciates you." Max tried to sound convincing. "I'm almost done with the corset for Tiffany's dress. There are only two grommets left to go. Her first fitting is tomorrow, so it would be great if you got it done today, regardless of what Darlene has you doing."

That got a big smile out of Keiko. "Don't worry. I'll get it done." Tiffany's dress was the first wedding gown Keiko had ever designed, and it was an imaginative fantasy-inspired gown for a non-traditional bride. Keiko's artwork and design skills had so impressed Max that she'd hired her on the spot when her boss went on vacation a few months ago. For someone who had just turned twenty-one, Keiko had a lot of skills, including being a whiz on the computer, but dress design was her passion. Max's dress construction skills allowed the two of them to make her designs a reality. Sometimes Max worried that working in a bridal shop wasn't enough of a challenge for Keiko. Maybe if Max had her own shop, she could find other projects for Keiko that she would find more inspiring.

They pulled into the parking lot of the Crystal

Shores Playhouse. The Playhouse had been converted from a church built in the 1920s, but the cobblestone walls made it appear as if it had been there forever. The parking lot overlooked the ocean and Keiko seemed lost in thought staring out at the water.

She turned to Max with a pleading look. "Do I have to go back?"

"Call me if you need me," Max said, getting out of the car. "Hang in there!"

"I won't quit today," Keiko teased. "Tiffany's fitting is tomorrow!"

"Okay, then." Max and Keiko had almost made a mantra out of 'I won't quit today.' It was their way of taking things one day at a time. The two of them loved working together, and that helped them put up with Darlene and her demands. "See you tonight!"

Max walked up the stone steps to the front of the theatre and pulled open the heavy wooden door, stepping into the lobby. The doors to the auditorium stood open, and she walked down the center aisle. Every step echoed in the silent theater as she tiptoed up the stairs to the stage. At the back of the stage, she pulled a curtain aside and walked down the hall toward the costume shop. The backstage area smelled of sawdust and history.

She noticed a door open and peeked inside. In the tiny room, a small, dark-haired man with sunken cheekbones sat at a desk.

"Hello," she said. "I'm Max. I'm here to help with the costumes.

"Max. That is an interesting name," he said, in a thick, Russian accent. "Is it short for Maxine?"

"No, it's not short for anything. It's just Max." She smiled as if it were the first time anyone had asked her that question. She didn't feel the need to confide in this stranger that she was pretty sure her parents expected a boy. Her late mother, an engineer, told her she named her after the physicist Max Plank, while her father, the artist, said she was named after Maxfield Parrish.

"And you are?" Max asked.

"My name is Ivan Petrov," the man said. "I am the director of this little production."

Max soon learned Ivan had no idea what needed to be done as far as the costumes were concerned. Apparently, no one had thought to prepare for the possibility Anastasia's baby might choose to arrive early.

Max walked down the narrow hallway to the costume shop, stepped inside, and surveyed the room. Two sewing machines sat in the center of the room along with a large wooden table covered with various multi-colored pieces of fabric. A sofa, covered in more swatches of fabric, took up most of one wall. Along the far wall were two racks full of costumes. The bare grey walls looked like they could use a coat of paint.

Max searched for a list that Anastasia might have kept of all the costumes. She finally found a notebook under a pile of fabric on the table. It listed each character with sketches of their various costumes. Thank goodness!

Looking more closely at the rack, she saw the

costumes were hung separated by tags with the character's names. Max said a silent thank you to Anastasia for being organized in spite of the room's appearance. She checked the costumes against the list in the notebook and found that all were there in various stages of completion.

A knock on the door made her look up, and she grimaced when Celeste Beidleman entered, but quickly recovered her composure. Celeste was her arch nemesis, or at least that's the way Max thought of her when they were in middle school together. Max remembered the pacifier tied to her locker and could almost hear Celeste and her clique calling out "crybaby," when they passed her in the hall. Max had never got over being angry with herself for letting them see her cry, but she could only take so much teasing. For years, Max had avoided Celeste, which was not too hard since they moved in different circles.

Max marveled at Celeste's perfect mocha colored skin, huge brown eyes, and full lips. How could someone so beautiful be so mean? She wore leggings and a form fitting tank top. Max caught a glimpse of what appeared to be a huge diamond on her left hand. Max had heard that Celeste had married a wealthy older man. If that diamond were any indication, then he must be quite well off.

"So, you're taking over." Celeste didn't wait for a response. "I'm so glad you're here. You were such a big help last time. I wish you could be our costumer instead of Anastasia."

Max didn't know what to say, unaccustomed to compliments from Celeste. She finally said, "Thanks. I heard you're playing Juliet." She supposed that twenty-seven wasn't necessarily too old to be playing the role of Juliet, but Celeste had a certain maturity about her. She'd always seemed older than her years, even back in middle school. Max wondered how believable Celeste would be playing a teenager.

"Yes, finally. I've been harping on Kenneth to do *Romeo and Juliet* for two years. I don't know what took him so long. He wanted to do *Macbeth* instead, but I'm much too young to play Lady Macbeth." Celeste walked over to the rack of costumes and pulled out a beautiful red gown with intricate gold trim. "Now, the first thing you need to work on is this dress." She handed it to Max. "I wear it in the first act. It squashes my boobs, making me look like a ten-year-old boy. Anastasia wasn't nearly as capable as you are."

Okay, this was getting a bit much. Did Celeste want something from her, besides a better fitting dress? Max wasn't a teenager anymore, and it was about time she said what was on her mind. "Why are you being so nice to me?' she asked, bluntly.

Celeste stood with her mouth open in surprise. Maybe she wasn't used to honesty. She closed her mouth and looked at the floor. "I was really mean to you in school, wasn't I?" she said meekly.

"Yes, you were. You made middle school miserable for me."

Celeste looked Max in the eyes and said, "I'm sorry."

"You're sorry? That's it? That's supposed to make everything better?" Max hated it when people thought that an apology was supposed to make up for whatever they'd done. The hurt didn't just disappear.

"I know I was a bully. I have no excuse for how I treated you. But I want to try to be a better person." When Max didn't respond, she reached out and took one of Max's hands in her own. She continued in a voice not much more than a whisper, "I might die soon."

"What?" Max wondered if she heard her right. "Are you ill?" Celeste looked the picture of health.

"Oh, no." She shook her head sadly. "Nothing like that. I saw Madam Giana. She's my psychic."

"You have a psychic?"

"Yes. She's really more of a spiritual guide. I went to see her the other night and she said some nut was going to kill me."

Max started to laugh but stopped when she saw the deadly serious look on Celeste's face. "You don't really believe that a psychic can tell you when you're going to die, do you?"

Celeste's eyes were wide with worry. "She's been right before. She told me I would lose someone close to me right before my mother died. Then, recently she told me that I would meet someone important from my past, and I have. I don't care if you believe me or not, but I need your help. You found a murderer before. I want you to find this one. Find them before they murder me."

Now Max had heard everything. She was supposed to figure out which nutcase was out to murder Celeste based on the word of a psychic? "I don't believe anyone can tell the future. There are too many variables."

"So, you won't help?" Celeste said in a mournful voice.

"You're really taking this seriously, aren't you?" When Celeste nodded, Max said, "Have you noticed anything strange or anyone acting differently?"

"The director, Ivan. There's something suspicious about him."

"Suspicious in what way?"

Celeste frowned. "I don't know. I tried to ask him where he was from, and he was very evasive. He seems to avoid me." She looked deep in thought. "And then there's the actor that plays Tybalt. I don't remember his name. He's always lurking about. He's up to something, I can tell you that."

"I tell you what," Max said to appease her, "I'll check around and see what I can find out."

"Thank you, Max," Celeste said, giving her an unexpected hug.

"Now, let's deal with something I know I can fix. Put the dress on, and I'll see what I can do with it."

Celeste undressed to her skimpy, expensive looking black bra and panties, and started to put the dress on.

"Don't you have a corset to wear with it?" Max asked. When Celeste shook her head, Max said, "That's the problem." Max knew that a corset could do wonders. She'd gone to the Renaissance Faire enough times to know that.

Celeste finished putting on the velvet dress, and Max zipped her up. Zippers weren't historically accurate, but they couldn't be seen from the audience, so she understood why Anastasia used them. Celeste looked stunning as she admired herself in the mirror. She had a point. There was no support built into the bodice.

"I think I saw some corsets in a drawer, and maybe one will fit you. Take the dress off and I'll measure you."

Celeste stood in her underwear with Max taking measurements when the door opened, and a handsome young man entered.

Max froze when she saw the stranger, but she quickly recovered, grabbed Celeste's costume and tried covering up Celeste with it. "Don't you knock?"

The man started to back out of the doorway when Celeste said, "It's okay, Max." She pushed the costume away. She didn't seem the least bit self-conscious about having a man in the room while she wore almost nothing.

"Max!" he said. "It's me, Brian Lovett. We were lab partners in chemistry class back in high school."

"Brian?" Max looked at him more closely. Her old lab partner was nearly unrecognizable. She remembered the chubby kid with glasses she'd known then. She hadn't realized he had gorgeous amber brown eyes framed by long eyelashes. His brown hair was closely cropped, not shaggy the way she remembered it. "Wow! I almost didn't recognize you." He may have not been handsome in high school, but he was one of the sweetest guys she knew, helping her get through their experiments so she could pass the class.

"You mean you didn't recognize me at all," he laughed. "I got laser eye surgery and lost some weight."

"And you're at the gym all the time," Celeste added. She stood close enough to touch him and she did, stroking the front of his shirt.

Brian seemed to ignore Celeste, though Max didn't know how he could ignore the scantily clad, gorgeous woman caressing him. He turned his back on her and said in a scolding voice, "Get dressed, why don't you?"

"I haven't seen you around since high school," Max said. "Where have you been keeping yourself?"

"I didn't go far. I've just been living in Laguna Beach. But I heard you were in New York for a while. Why did you come back?"

"My mom was ill, so I came back to be with her. I almost went back to New York a few months ago, but I decided I was happy right where I was."

"We need to get together and catch up." He turned and spoke to Celeste, who was still in her underwear. "Put on your clothes. I want to rehearse the balcony scene before everyone else arrives."

"You're in the play?" Max asked, finally figuring out why her old classmate was there. He explained he had been cast as Romeo.

"Hold on," Celeste ordered. "We're in the middle of a fitting."

Max went to the drawer with the corsets and pulled out one. She helped Celeste into the corset and dress.

Celeste looked breathtaking in the voluminous dress with a good portion of her breasts pushed up over the top of the bodice. She grinned and admired herself some more in the mirror.

"You're a genius, Max!"

Max was stunned. She didn't know what to think about the way Celeste was treating her. Maybe she really had changed.

"I'll see you later, Max," Brian said, giving her a wink. He grabbed Celeste's hand and led her back out into the theater.

"Wait," Max called out, but they were gone. Celeste would be the only actor in costume.

Brian and Celeste made a cute couple. Except for the fact that Celeste was married.

CHAPTER 3

By six o'clock most of the actors had arrived for rehearsal. Fiona McNulty, one of the owners of the Knitpickers yarn store, had been cast in the role of Juliet's nurse and stopped in to say hello. She wore her trademark bedazzled baseball cap along with an oversized Angel's t-shirt and black leggings. Today's sneakers were red to match the t-shirt. She had a collection in nearly every color. Between the yarn shop and community theater, she kept busy since she'd retired from her job as a high school principal.

"So, Kenneth talked you into helping, I see." Fiona put her hands on her sturdy hips.

"It's more like Darlene ordered me," Max said. "Have you heard if Anastasia had her baby yet?"

"False alarm. But the doctor has her on bed rest. So, it looks like you're stuck here with us for a while."

"I don't mind too much," Max said, thinking that at least it got her away from Darlene for a while. Why had Darlene been so short with her lately? Was it something she'd done? She knew she should bring it up with Darlene, but she hated confrontation. She preferred to hope her boss's mood would improve on its own.

Max pulled Fiona's costume from the rack. "How have rehearsals been going?"

"Pretty smooth, in spite of our prima donna and all her demands. That girl is a handful."

"Yes, I've already run into Celeste. She was actually nice to me." Max inspected Fiona's costume.

"Don't expect that to last. She can only be nice in small doses, but she has been nicer lately. I think it's because she's in love. You should see the way she looks at Romeo. Although, it may be just lust. Sometimes, it's hard to tell the difference."

"True. They did seem pretty friendly, especially considering the fact that she's married. Would you try this on for me?" Max held the voluminous white nurse's dress over Fiona's head so she could slip into it.

"I forget at times that you know everyone in town," Fiona said from under all the fabric.

"Not everyone," Max admitted. "I never met Ivan, the director, before."

"He's not from here, that's why." Fiona poked her head out of the top of the dress. "He's a piece of work, I'll tell you."

"What do you mean?" Max asked.

"He acts like he's directing a Broadway show. I reminded him that this is community theater, and he just sneered at me. I think this is a step down for him. Or at least he acts like it is."

Fiona's costume needed very little work, thank

goodness. Once Max sewed the hem, it would be done, so she began pinning it up while Fiona shared more gossip. Celeste's husband, George, was helping to fund the production, and he often showed up for rehearsals. Celeste seemed especially petulant when he visited, which Fiona surmised was because she couldn't hang all over Brian with her husband watching.

While they were talking, someone knocked on the door, and Olivia Cavendish entered. She was the resident stage manager and one of Max's closest friends.

"I'm so happy to have you here," Olivia told Max, giving her a hug. "Anastasia was a competent seamstress, but there were a number of issues with the costumes that she didn't have the skills to handle. You've already improved Celeste's dress, and I'm thrilled she has one less thing to complain about. She loves it so much she doesn't want to take it off." She took the pincushion from Max and started handing her pins as Max continued to work on the hem of Fiona's costume. "I hope you don't mind the long hours between working at the bridal shop and here. Have you figured out how much is left to do before we open next Friday?"

"There's quite a bit. It's going to be a lot of work, but it's a nice change of pace," Max said. "Still, ask me again in a few days and I may have a different attitude." Seeing Olivia had cheered her up. Maybe it would be fun working at the theater temporarily, instead of with grumpy Darlene, assuming she could get everything done in time.

"It will certainly be a change of pace for you," Olivia

said. "The theater is a different world. There's more drama than one of your mystery books."

"Boy," Fiona piped in, "she's not kidding."

"Really? What kind of drama?" Max wondered.

"Oh, romances, jealousy, ego trips," Fiona said.

Olivia agreed. "Plus, I always have actors coming to complain to me that they have to kiss another actor with bad breath or who sweats too much. I've even had actors complain that a kissing scene went too far. Kenneth doesn't like to have those conversations, so I'm the one who gets to deal with it."

There was another knock on the door and Max called out. "Come in! The more the merrier!"

Keiko had come straight from the shop. She said she'd come to help, but then told Max, Olivia and Fiona about how Darlene had criticized Tiffany's dress. Max continued to pin Fiona's hem while Keiko talked. Keiko seemed on the verge of tears.

"Keiko," Max said firmly. "Darlene doesn't get it. It doesn't matter what she thinks. The only thing that matters is what Tiffany thinks."

Keiko gave Max a smile. "You're right. It's just that it's my first design and I'm so nervous about Tiffany seeing it for the first time tomorrow."

"She loved your sketch, right?" When Keiko nodded, Max said, "She's going to absolutely love the dress."

"I hope so. No, I'm sure of it." Keiko's normal confidence was back.

Max asked her, "Feel better?"

Keiko laughed. "Yes, much. Thanks, Max. Sorry, everyone, for complaining."

Fiona said, "I understand, Keiko. Darlene is a friend of mine, but only because I don't have to work for her. I can give her a piece of my mind when I feel the need." Fiona gave a piece of her mind to anyone she thought deserved it. "By the way, I want to thank you again for our website. Sales are up again this week."

"You don't need to thank me every time sales go up," Keiko said, but had a big grin on her face. "You paid me for my work."

"We should have paid you double."

"Just tell everyone you know, and I'll charge them double," Keiko said happily.

"I like the way you think!" Fiona said.

Max told Fiona she could take off her costume. Max thought it looked adorable with the baseball cap, but she had a sudden thought. Fiona's short grey hair wasn't exactly appropriate for the period of the play. "Are you going to be wearing a wig?"

"No, I'm supposed to be wearing some kind of a head scarf. I forget what it's called." She changed back into her street clothes.

"It's called a coif," Olivia said.

"Great." Max sighed. "I didn't see anything like that in her notes. Just one more thing for me to figure out. Thank goodness for the Internet."

Olivia left to let Max and Keiko get to work and Fiona helped out by folding fabric and putting it all in a neat pile on the table, sharing more gossip. Fiona seemed to have an endless supply, and Max only half listened while she sewed at the machine. Keiko searched online for instructions on how to make a coif.

"And that's why we think Celeste was raised by wolves," Fiona concluded.

"What?" Max looked up from her work.

"Oh, so you were listening. Just checking." Fiona folded the last piece of fabric. "I think I'll go check on the rehearsal and leave you to your work."

Before she could leave there was another knock on the door and Brian entered. Max pretended to pay attention to the dress she was in the middle of sewing. Handsome men always made her nervous. She'd never been nervous around him back in high school when he was her lab partner.

"Hello, ladies," he said in greeting. "Notice how I knocked this time?" he said to Max, and she looked up and smiled at him. "Celeste's husband just showed up, so she's sweet talking him. I'm happy to get a break from her."

"You looked like you were getting along great earlier," Fiona said. "In fact, you were downright friendly."

"So, you've noticed her coming on to me?" he said, frowning. "It's a bit much to handle."

"You didn't look like you were suffering too much," Fiona said, not mincing words.

"From what I've heard, she always flirts with her leading men. She thinks it helps our onstage chemistry. I'd tell her to back off, but she's got Kenneth wrapped around her finger. You'd think she had something on Kenneth, the way he goes along with all her demands, but maybe it's just because her husband is helping fund the show. I'm afraid if I told her to leave me alone, she'd have me fired. After this play I'll have enough points to get my equity card, so I really need this job."

Max wondered if community theater was always this gossipy. Did they all know and share each other's secrets?

Celeste burst in without knocking. "There you are," she said to Brian in a sultry voice. "Enough goofing off. Kenneth has sent all the other actors home besides you and me and our understudies. Let's get back to rehearsing the balcony scene, and I hope you can remember your lines this time."

After Celeste and Brian left, Fiona said to Max and Keiko, "I'm not buying it. As Shakespeare would say, 'He doth protest too much.' If you ask me, he's enjoying the attention from that woman. Even if they're not having an affair yet, there's been some hanky panky going on. I'm sure of it."

Fiona was the only person who could say hanky panky and make it sound convincing.

A loud crash came from the theater. The three women looked at each other and then rushed out the door, down the hall, and onto the stage.

At the bottom of the balcony, Celeste lay still and unmoving in the beautiful crimson velvet dress.

CHAPTER 4

Max ran onto the stage and saw all the actors staring at Celeste lying on the stage floor. One of the older male actors who looked familiar leaned down over her lifeless body calling out to no one in particular, "Someone call 911!"

Fiona told everyone to move back, and the actors and workers stood around staring and murmuring.

Celeste's eyes were open, and her neck was twisted in an unnatural way. For a moment, Max couldn't tear her eyes away. Then she looked up at the balcony where Celeste must have stood moments before. She moved closer to the balcony. A piece of wood that had formerly been part of the top railing was hanging down loose. Not splintered as if it had broken, but intact as if it had just come apart. Had someone built a flimsy balcony? Everyone else was still focused on Celeste and didn't notice Max except for Keiko, who walked over to her and whispered in her ear.

"She's dead, isn't she?" Keiko asked.

Max looked back at Celeste. Fiona crouched next to her lifeless body and began administering CPR following the instructions coming from Kenneth's phone. She looked sadly at Keiko and said nothing, but she hoped Keiko was wrong. There had been too much death in her life lately.

What a tragic accident. It seemed unlikely that someone had tried to murder Celeste, since no one could be sure that she would die from an eight-foot fall. In fact, it seemed more likely that she would have been injured. Maybe she shouldn't wonder about foul play every time someone died, but she couldn't help herself, especially after one of her clients was murdered just a few months ago.

Fiona continued to administer CPR while Brian paced anxiously nearby. The other actors stood staring in a wide circle around Celeste. A young slender actress with long straight blonde hair pulled Brian aside and whispered in his ear. He shook his head and walked away from her.

Sirens howled in the distance, getting louder and louder until they finally stopped. The front doors of the theater opened, and two paramedics dashed up the aisle and onto the stage. The male ordered everyone to step back. He and another female paramedic busied themselves with Celeste's lifeless body.

A uniformed officer came in and walked over to the paramedics who whispered to him before putting Celeste on a stretcher and carrying her to their ambulance.

"Who's in charge here?" The officer asked.

"I am," Kenneth said. His lined face and grey hair gave him an air of dignity, but now he looked stunned. "I'm the artistic director."

Max tried to hear what they were saying, but everyone was talking, wondering if Celeste would be okay and asking each other questions that no one had answers for.

Max moved closer to the balcony and peered up at the railings. She took a picture with her phone so she could blow it up and take a better look. Two rails spanned the length of the small balcony. The lower one was intact, but the upper one was hanging down on one side, as if the bolts or nails that held it together had come loose. Celeste must have been leaning over the balcony when it came apart.

The uniformed officer came over to her. "What are you doing?" he asked.

Max showed him the enlarged picture on her phone. "It looks to me like the railing came apart."

The officer called into his station and talked to someone in charge. Max overheard him say his name was Officer Daniels.

Max turned when she heard Kenneth, his voice booming to get the group's attention. "Go home, everyone," he announced. "We'll meet back here tomorrow at six. I'm sure we'll know more about Celeste by then."

Keiko appeared by Max's side, tugging at Max's sleeve. "Let's go home," she said.

Before Max could turn to follow her, Officer Daniels announced, "I need to ask everyone to wait just a few more minutes. You'll be able to leave shortly."

The officer talked to Kenneth, but Max couldn't hear what they said over everyone else's talking. She gave up and she and Keiko found ornate chairs to sit in on one side of the stage.

"What's going on?" Keiko asked. "Why can't we leave?"

"I don't know," Max answered, but she knew someone was to blame for Celeste's fall. It was likely negligence, but the police would have to investigate. Max couldn't help but think about Celeste's premonition. Had she been killed like the psychic said?

It wasn't long before the front door opened, and Detective Jason Cruz walked up the center aisle toward the stage. Max's heart skipped a beat when she saw him. Of course, he would be here—she should have expected it. What she didn't expect was to feel like a shy schoolgirl after not seeing him for several months. Was the tall, dark-haired detective always this handsome?

He had arrived with a young woman who Max assumed was CSI. He headed toward Kenneth, surveying the surroundings, and then he saw Max. Did she imagine that his face lit up when their eyes met? His mouth opened as if about to say something, then he regained his composure and walked up to Kenneth.

Detective Cruz and Kenneth talked for several minutes, then the detective climbed the stairs to the balcony and inspected the railing that had failed.

Max waited for him at the bottom of the stairs. "Hello, Detective Cruz," she called up to him. She walked up a few steps before he held out a hand, motioning for her to stop.

"What are you doing here?" he asked, to the point, as usual.

"Nice to see you, too. The railing seems to have come apart." She tried to talk quietly so no one else heard. The others didn't seem to be paying attention to them anyway, except for Keiko, who watched closely from below. "Do you suppose it could have come loose by itself?"

"All these bolts are loose," he said, almost to himself. He looked at Max and added, "Don't say anything to anyone. I don't need people to be pointing fingers at each other until I've collected all the evidence."

"Lashari," he called out to the CSI as he was climbing down the stairs. When he got to the bottom, he quietly told her, "Look for bolts or any kind of hardware." The dark-haired woman scoured the floor, carefully looking but finding nothing.

Max watched carefully, wondering why the bolts would have been left so loose that they would have come out on their own. Who would be so careless?

Detective Cruz addressed all the actors who were watching his every move. "Did anyone see any hardware on the floor?" When no one answered, he added, "Bolts or screws or anything like that?"

The blonde actress spoke up. "I found this. Is this what you're talking about?" She pulled a bolt out of her pocket. "I tripped on it and nearly fell. There's always stuff lying around on the stage, so I didn't think anything of it. I didn't want someone else to trip on it."

The uniformed officer pulled out a plastic bag and asked the actress to place it inside.

"And your name is?" Cruz asked.

"Heather Lamarque. I'm the understudy for Juliet." She paused. "For Celeste. She's going to be okay, isn't she?"

"We'll let everyone know as soon as we have more information about her condition," Cruz said, and then instructed Officer Daniels to sequester the witnesses until he could question them. Daniels herded the actors plus Kenneth, Olivia, Max, and Keiko into Kenneth's office to wait. They stood shoulder to shoulder in the small room, while Kenneth sat behind his desk. He pulled out a bottle of vodka and some paper cups and passed out drinks, which all of the actors accepted. Kenneth poured himself a stiff one. Max politely refused, wanting to keep a clear head.

Max stood between Keiko and Fiona, observing each of the people in the room. Kenneth seemed calm in spite of what had just happened. Heather kept glancing at Brian, who stared at the floor. Behind her stood Brian's understudy. Max now recognized the older man who had taken Celeste's pulse. It was Peter Nilsson, a friend of her father's. She wondered what he was doing here.

Fiona leaned close to Max and quietly asked why they were being questioned, but Max just shrugged. "I suppose it's routine," she said.

Officer Daniels stood blocking the door with his arms crossed over his muscular chest.

"Hey, where's Ivan?" Brian asked.

"He never showed up," Kenneth said. "He usually gets here around 6:30."

"Isn't that when she fell?" Brian finished his vodka in one gulp and threw the cup in the trash.

Max said, "She fell around 6:28." When everyone looked at her, she added, "I looked up at the clock when I heard the crash."

Heather turned to Peter. "This is your fault. You built most of the set. You and Nathan."

Peter's jaw dropped. "How can you say a thing like that? I would never do anything to put Celeste in danger." His eyes glistened. Was he fighting back tears? "You know how I felt about her."

"You hardly knew her," Heather snapped. "I was her friend. Probably the only friend she had at this theater. I heard what everyone said about her."

Max wasn't surprised that Celeste didn't have many friends, but she would like to know more about what people had said. Maybe she could question Heather in private.

A small voice behind Max said, "I saw her fall."

Max turned around. Brian's understudy met her eyes and then looked away. "Are you okay?" she asked. His face was pale.

"It was like slow motion. She was leaning over the railing and then it gave way. She looked surprised and then she screamed. When she hit the ground-" he stopped talking, unable to continue.

Heather was at his side and enveloped him in a hug. "It's okay, Tim. It's all going to be okay."

The young man protested. "I'm fine." Clearly, he wasn't. Fighting back tears, he repeated, "I'm fine."

"When are we getting out of here?" Peter asked no one in particular.

"There's a good chance it's going to be a long night," Max said. "The police are probably going to want to question all of us."

"What are you talking about?" Brian said, scowling at her. "Why are we all being questioned about an accident?"

"They have to figure out what happened." Max had no reason to think it was anything but an accident, but she couldn't help but wonder if someone might have sabotaged the balcony. Was she feeling this way just because Celeste had said someone would kill her? "Detective Cruz will be investigating even if it is just an unfortunate accident."

The door opened and the officer stepped aside so Detective Cruz could enter.

"I just got a call from the hospital," he said. "Celeste was pronounced dead on arrival."

Several people gasped. Keiko grabbed Max's arm. "I knew it," she whispered.

Cruz announced, "There will be an autopsy, but in the meantime, I'll need to question each of you. I'll do my best to get everyone out of here as soon as possible." He motioned to Max. "Would you come with me?"

Max gladly followed Detective Cruz out of the stuffy room and next door to Olivia's office. She sat down in an armchair, and he took his place behind Olivia's desk, notebook in hand. He clicked his pen while she waited for him to begin. The habit irritated her, but other than that, Detective Cruz seemed perfect, with his green eyes and the way his tailored dark grey suit emphasized his muscular shoulders. She sucked in her breath and tried to concentrate. Surely, he had faults other than one annoying habit. For one thing, he liked to do things by the book, but that was probably an asset for a police detective.

He didn't wear a wedding ring, but not all married men wore one. Maybe he had a girlfriend, though he'd never mentioned it. But then, it wasn't as if they talked about their personal lives with each other. And she hadn't seen him at all since he saved her from a homicidal maniac four months ago.

"Have you called her husband and her parents?" Max asked. "I mean her dad?" Celeste's mother had passed away a few years ago.

"Yes, they've been notified." He leaned forward and put his pen down. He ran one hand over his hair as if to smooth it, although not a strand was ever out of place. Was that another nervous habit? "We'll be taking everyone's fingerprints, but since Heather touched the bolt, I don't know if we'll be able to pull any other fingerprints off of it. Right now, it looks like an accident. We'll be investigating to see who's at fault."

"If it was an accident, I hope Nathan won't be held liable," Max said.

"Kenneth already told me that Nathan Cutter built the set. I don't suppose I should be surprised that you know him."

"Nathan's very professional," she said, "and I don't

believe that he would leave a loose bolt. Did you know he works for Beidleman Construction? Celeste's husband owns it."

"That's interesting." He paused as if thinking over the new information. "I'll have to question him, but it looks like two bolts came out and the railing failed. With all the bolts left so loose, it's not surprising. I'll find out who's responsible. And maybe this time you'll leave the investigating to me."

She knew he was just doing his job, but she didn't appreciate him being condescending to her after she solved the last murder in town. She might not have his experience or training, but she had a knack for figuring things out and a curiosity that wouldn't let her stay out of it.

He seemed to think her lack of response was agreement and went into his investigating mode. "Did you know Celeste well?"

"We went to school together." Max told him about how Celeste tormented her, calling her a baby after making her cry and encouraging her friends to tease her as well. "But then, she was mean to pretty much everyone back then, except the popular kids. Until today, I'd barely seen her in the past eight or nine years, but I don't think she was any more well liked than she was back then."

"That doesn't make it murder," the detective said.

"No, I wasn't implying anything. But there's something else."

"What's that?" he asked, his pen poised to write down the new information.

"Well," she began, hoping she didn't sound silly, "Celeste told me tonight that a psychic warned her that she would be killed."

He put his pen and pad down on the desk. He rubbed his temples as if he were trying to fend off a headache. "A psychic? You believe in psychics?"

"No, of course not. But Celeste certainly did." She saw the weary look on his face. "I just thought you should know."

"Okay," he said, picking up his pad and pen again. "What was her name?"

"It was Madam Ganna or something like that. So, you'll be questioning her?"

"Yes, if I can locate her. First, I need to question everyone here tonight and anyone else who might have been involved."

"Great, let's get to work, shall we?"

"We?" Detective Cruz shook his head. Max hoped he realized it would be futile to fight the inevitable. She would help him solve the case, whether it was an accident or not. Was the psychic right? Had she been murdered?

CHAPTER 5

Shortly before nine, everyone had been questioned and allowed to leave. Max sent Keiko home, and after calling her father for a ride, went back to the costume shop. Detective Cruz stopped in to say goodnight and told her that her dad had arrived and was talking to Kenneth.

Someone knocked on the door and she looked up, expecting to see her father. Instead, Peter Nilsson entered. He'd grown a goatee since she last saw him, which explained why she hadn't recognized him right away.

She asked him why he was at the theater, and he explained that he was playing Friar Laurence. With his silver hair, he was perfect for the role.

"Long day, huh?" he said. Huge understatement. She took the dress she was working on out of the sewing machine and leaned back in her chair.

"Well, technically, they're all the same length," she

joked. "Twenty-four hours. At least that's one thing that hasn't changed."

"Not yet," Peter said, walking over to her and leaning in for a hug. "Wait till they come out with Day 2.0. Somebody will figure out how to fit an extra hour or two in there."

"As long as I get to do absolutely nothing for the extra time. Or sleep. More sleep would be good."

"More sleep is always good."

Max thought he hadn't come in to talk to her about sleeping, but she waited for him to get to the point.

"I hope you'll find out who murdered Celeste."

"Maybe it was just an accident," Max said, trying to sound convincing.

"Maybe, but if it wasn't an accident, I want to know who's responsible. Hell, even if it was an accident, I want to know whose fault it was."

"Detective Cruz is very capable. I'm sure he'll get to the bottom of it." She'd rather not tell everyone that she was doing her own investigation. Although, in this small town, secrets were hard to keep.

"Okay, but you found the last murderer. I can't believe our little town is faced with another suspicious death so soon. Please say you'll help."

"It sounds like you care about her." This surprised Max, but then she thought maybe Celeste really had changed since high school. Besides, even mean girls had people who cared about them. But Peter was much older than Celeste. It seemed odd that he had developed such a close attachment to her.

"I do. I did." He blinked back tears and stared at the

floor. "During the past several weeks, I'd spent a lot of time with her." He must have noticed Max's quizzical look. "She was…" he paused, as if he were about to say something but changed his mind. He blinked back tears. "She was like a daughter to me." He looked up at Max and laughed softly. "Like a difficult, teenage daughter, but all the same, I tried to look after her. And I failed."

Max stood up and gave him a long hug. "I'm so sorry for your loss."

Max let him talk about Celeste while she waited for her dad. The sewing could wait.

"Celeste was an insecure young woman." He obviously saw the dubious look on Max's face, because he said, "No, really. She needed constant reassurance about her looks and her acting abilities. She was terrified of getting older, afraid that her husband would find a younger wife."

"But she was only twenty-seven." Just a year older than Max. Max worried about a lot of things but getting older wasn't one of them.

"Her husband left his thirty-year-old wife for Celeste when she was just nineteen. She's afraid he'll do it again." Peter frowned. "Personally, I thought she'd be better off without him if all he cared about was her youth and beauty."

"Maybe she stayed because of the money," Max suggested.

"No, Celeste came from money. She didn't need his. She never worked in her life. Didn't need to. The theater was everything to her."

Max remembered the beautiful clothes Celeste wore when they went to school together and she'd even visited her parents' house once, for the disastrous pool party when Celeste and her friends had teased her until she cried.

"Do you know why she never had kids?"

Peter shook his head. "I don't think she believed she would make a good mother. I told her that being a parent changes you."

"I didn't know you had kids," Max said, surprised.

"Oh, I don't. I'm not speaking from personal experience." He got up to leave. "Has someone told her husband?"

"Yes, he's been notified," Max said.

"I wonder how he took it."

Max wondered the same thing. Had George Beidleman witnessed Celeste flirting with Brian? What if he were the jealous type? Nathan, the set builder, worked for him. Maybe she should arrange to talk to Nathan.

After Peter left, Max wondered why he seemed to care so much about Celeste. He'd started to say, "She was..." and she was quite sure he was going to say something else before he said, "like a daughter." What had he started to say and why had he changed his mind?

~

MAX KNEW HER DAD WOULD HAVE A FEW THINGS TO SAY on the drive home.

"This time, you're going to let the police handle it, right?" Richard Walters had always worried about his only daughter, but after the last murderer had held her at gunpoint, he worried even more. Max had proved she could take care of herself, and he needed to treat her more like a grownup. But even though it annoyed her when he was overprotective, it was kind of sweet.

"Dad, it looks like it was an unfortunate accident," she said, hoping to ease his mind. "I'm not in any danger."

"Just a few months ago you were nearly killed. I don't need to stay awake at night worrying about you. I can't think about losing you. You're all I have." He drove in silence, and Max knew he was thinking about the wife who'd lost the battle to cancer less than a year ago.

"I miss Mom, too." She reached over and patted his shoulder. If he weren't driving, she would have hugged him. He was all the family she had, as well.

"I'm just going to tell Detective Cruz everything I know and let him bounce ideas off me. He seems to like doing that." She wanted to stay safe, but she also wanted to find out what happened to Celeste. She hoped she could do both.

"I suppose so," he said gruffly and pulled his Mini Cooper into a spot between two SUVs in front of the house. "Want some hot chocolate?" When Max shook her head, he said, "Something stronger? I know you've had a long day."

"No kidding. I think I'm just going to call it a night."

She followed her dad into his house, taking a short cut to the back yard. "Dad, how often do you see Peter?"

"Pretty often. He's one of my best friends. Why do you ask?"

"Did he talk to you about Celeste?"

Richard didn't answer right away. "He cared a lot about her," he finally said.

"Why?" she asked. It didn't make sense to her that a fifty-something single man and a 27- year-old married woman had become so close. When he didn't answer, she prodded, "Well?"

"It's really not my place to say anything," Richard said. He walked into the kitchen and poured himself a glass of wine.

Max's intuition was working overtime. "She's his daughter, isn't she?"

"What?" Richard said, dumbfounded. "How did you figure that out?"

"It was a guess, but you just confirmed it. Pour me a glass of that wine, too. I'm suddenly wide awake."

Richard told her that Celeste's mother had sent Peter a letter written on her deathbed, telling him that Celeste was his daughter. That was why Peter had moved to Crystal Shores, but he hadn't said anything to Celeste until he realized what a terrible relationship she had with the man she thought was her father. He'd asked Richard for advice, and he told Peter to show Celeste the letter. It took him months to get up the nerve, but he'd finally done it just a few weeks ago.

"How did she take it?" Max wondered.

"She was thrilled. The man she thought was her

father had always been cold and distant with her, and she never understood why. It turns out he knew she wasn't his daughter. Knowing that she had a father who loved her filled a hole in her life."

Max's heart warmed to think that Celeste had found out about her father before she died. If Peter had waited a little longer, she never would have known.

"How did Peter know Celeste's mother? Did Peter live here back then?"

"They went to college together in San Diego." Richard said. "Celeste's mother left college, moved back to Crystal Shores, and married her high school sweetheart. She told Peter she didn't want to see him anymore. He never knew about the baby."

"So, he missed out on seeing his only child grow up. That's sad." And then he had lost her. "But I'm glad he didn't wait any longer to tell her."

Richard nodded, and Max knew he was thinking about Peter. She hoped he wasn't thinking about how it would feel to lose your only daughter.

Max finished her wine and gave her dad a long hug. She walked out the back door and up the stairs to her apartment over the garage. She loved coming home to her little place with its hardwood floors and big windows that let in plenty of light. No one could see in so she didn't even need drapes and she could leave the windows open on a warm night like tonight.

She hoped that, as exhausted as she was, she'd fall asleep quickly, but as soon as she put on her pajamas and climbed into bed, she knew she wouldn't get any sleep until she wrote everything down.

She got out of bed and found a spiral notebook and a pen. She wrote down the names of everyone who had been at the theater plus Nathan, Ivan, and Celeste's husband George. Any one of them could have removed a couple of bolts, since the stage was empty during the day, but who had a motive? Celeste flirted openly with Brian. Had her husband seen them together? Would he be angry enough to kill? Max thought he'd kill Brian before he'd kill his own wife.

But what if it wasn't murder? What if it was meant to be an accident? That certainly seemed more likely, since the chances of dying from a ten-foot fall were very unlikely. Who would have wanted to injure Celeste, maybe get her out of the play? Heather would get to play Juliet. Did she want the part that bad?

Nathan had a good reputation as a carpenter, but maybe he left the bolts loose. If that were true, that meant it was just an unfortunate accident. Someone would no doubt be held liable, whether it was Nathan or the theater. Max realized it could ruin Nathan if he was found at fault, since he'd probably be sued and lose both his reputation and his life savings.

Max could barely keep her eyes open, so she climbed back into bed. Her thoughts turned to Detective Cruz. Would he accept her help this time after she'd solved the last murder? Her last thought before she fell asleep was that she would be spending more time with the handsome, green-eyed detective.

CHAPTER 6

The phone rang much too early. Max opened one eye. The alarm clock said 7:00. Who would be calling her at this ungodly hour? She reached for the phone and saw Eric's name on the screen.

"Are you up?" his cheerful voice asked.

She grunted. "I am now, I guess. How can you be so perky at this hour?"

He laughed, but she didn't see why. "I've been up for an hour. The day is wasting away, girl. Get up and make yourself look pretty. I've made us an appointment at lunchtime to look at the space in Newport Beach I told you about for your shop."

"Maybe this isn't the best day to do this. I've got a lot on my mind. Did you hear about Celeste?"

"Yeah, we're going to talk about that later. I can't believe you didn't call me. I'll pick you up at Wedding Belles at noon. Now, get ready for work."

Max ignored his suggestion and fell back asleep. She didn't have to be at work until ten, so it was way too early to get up. She hit the snooze alarm one too many times. Or maybe three. When you're not a morning person and you stayed up late the night before making a list of suspects and motives, an hour to get ready isn't as much time as you might think. Max stumbled into the shower and after ten minutes in the hot water she started to feel human again. There would be no time for a morning walk along the beach. Looking through her closet for something appropriate to wear, she picked out one of the dresses she'd bought at a Melrose boutique on an outing with Keiko to L.A. The bright colors lifted her spirits. She put on her practical black sweater, which Keiko hadn't been able to make her give up yet, and walked down the stairs, across the back patio, and through the back door of her dad's house.

Coffee and oatmeal were ready, as usual, since Richard always set it up the night before. Whoever came up with the idea of making oatmeal in a rice cooker was brilliant. She crept through the silent house, checking to see if he had awakened yet. As an artist, he could make his own hours, and sometimes inspiration kept him painting late into the night. Max poured herself a cup of coffee and tiptoed into his workroom. An oil painting leaned on an easel. She stared at the translucent blue-green waves and could almost hear the crash as they hit the shore. She was in awe of her father's skill. Staring at one of his paintings felt almost like being there. No wonder tourists from the Midwest wanted to bring a Richard Walters painting home with them. Not that he didn't sell plenty to people in Crystal Shores and neighboring towns, but tourist season always gave him a big jump in sales.

She had settled down at the kitchen table with her coffee and oatmeal, when she looked up to see her father enter the room. He stretched and mumbled a greeting, going straight for the coffee. Once he sat down across from her and had a few sips of coffee, he seemed to be more awake.

"What would the world be like without coffee?" he asked.

"A lot sleepier. And grumpier. Were you up late?"

"After you went to bed, I stayed up working and lost track of time. I seem to do that a lot lately." Now that his eyes were fully open, he took a long look at her. "You look like you have something on your mind."

"You can always see right through me." It used to bother her when she was a teenager. She could never get away with anything. "I'm thinking of opening my own bridal shop."

"Well, that's exciting!" He grinned, and then gave her one of her fatherly looks. "Are you ready for that?"

"Eric has offered to be my investor. I haven't made a decision yet, but I'm seriously considering it."

"You sure have a lot going on," he said. "Are they going through with the play after what happened to Celeste?"

Celeste. She'd almost forgotten. It seemed wrong somehow, to feel happy and excited about opening her own shop when Celeste had just died. "I haven't heard anything one way or the other." She and Richard sat in silence, each in their own thoughts while they finished their breakfasts.

Max walked to work not noticing the beautiful flowers, cloudless blue sky or twittering birds. Her mind was on Celeste and whether someone might have wanted to harm her. She arrived at the shop five minutes before ten, let herself in, and locked the door behind her. Darlene would unlock it at ten sharp. You could set your watch by it. Well, if anyone wore watches anymore.

Max peeked in the office and said hello to Darlene. She stood in the doorway until her boss looked up.

"So, Kenneth told you what happened last night?" Max already knew the answer.

"Of course, he told me," Darlene snapped. "What did you expect?"

Max sighed. Sometimes she wondered why she even tried making conversation with Darlene. "It's sad. I mean, we weren't exactly friends, but it's still sad."

"I never knew the woman. She went to L.A. for her bridal gown. I guess we weren't good enough for her, in spite of the fact that we carry all the top designers."

Max went into the workroom to get started on her day. Tiffany would be stopping in for a fitting at eleven, so Max pulled her gown off the hanger and took one more look to see that everything was perfect. Tiffany's gown had been designed to be, at her request, "something an elfin princess would wear." Keiko had designed it, and Max had helped her make it a reality. Keiko was even more excited about it than the bride-to-be. She planned to come to work early so she could be there for the fitting.

She heard Darlene unlock the front door and knew it was ten o'clock. She heard voices and went out into the showroom to greet their client. Alicia, their ten o'clock appointment, had brought her mother for her first visit to try on wedding gowns.

Alicia arrived in leggings and a hoodie with her brown hair pulled back in a ponytail. Max couldn't wait to see the transformation they were about to make. Alicia's mom, whose hair was accented with carefully placed highlights, didn't look a day over forty, but many women—and men—didn't look their age in this town. There were probably more plastic surgeons per capita there than anywhere else in the country. Then there were the long-time residents like Darlene and Fiona who didn't mind looking their ages but felt that they had earned every wrinkle.

Max sat in on the consultation but kept quiet. Darlene preferred to ask all the questions. Darlene's consultations were always much quicker than hers. Max liked to ask more questions, because the more she learned about the bride the fewer dresses she'd have to pull. Max studied Alicia's fresh young face as she answered Darlene's questions, trying to learn the truth behind her answers. More than once, she said she liked a dress in a picture that Darlene showed her, but her face said something different.

"Pull some dresses and bring them into the Dream Room," Darlene said finally. Max smiled because

Darlene had finally started using her name for the mirrored area off the dressing room.

Max quickly pulled a dress off the rack and brought it to Darlene. She always wondered whether she should wait to bring in the perfect dress until after the client had tried on two or three dresses, but her impatience always made her want to give the bride-to-be the perfect dress first. Sometimes, they still had to try on several others to make sure, but usually the client picked the first dress.

"How many times do I have to tell you?" Darlene scolded her. "Three to five dresses."

"Just have her start with this one," Max said. "I'll get more." Darlene was stuck in her habits, and it was unlikely that she would ever let Max do things her way.

Max had a feeling it didn't matter what other dresses she pulled off the rack. Ten minutes later, she walked in with three more dresses, only to find Alicia and her mother in tears.

"It's perfect!" Alicia said, jumping off the platform in the wedding gown Max had picked out. She hugged Max. Her mother couldn't speak. Max wondered how long it had been since she'd seen her little girl in a dress.

Max brought several headdresses into the Dream Room for Alicia to try on, and they had picked out one together when they heard the front door make its friendly jingle. Darlene went into the front room and returned moments later.

"There's someone to see you."

Was Tiffany early? Max hoped not, since Keiko

would be very disappointed if she missed the fitting. She walked into the showroom, and there stood Detective Cruz. She wished her stomach didn't do a flip-flop every time she saw him. She didn't think police detectives should be so handsome. It was very distracting. She could get lost in his green eyes if she let herself, so it was a good thing she was able to exercise self-control.

"May we use the office?" Max asked Darlene, who frowned, then nodded without a word.

Max sat behind the desk and offered Cruz a seat across from her. Once the detective settled into the flowered chair, he took out a small notebook and pen. He clicked the pen the way he did the night before, and Max suppressed an urge to grab it from him. Was he nervous? She couldn't imagine why he'd be nervous talking to her.

Max got right to the point. "What's the latest on the case?"

"I came to tell you Celeste's death has been ruled an accident by the coroner." The detective sounded very official and emotionless.

"An accident?" She had known that this was a possibility, but she was still surprised. Her gut told her that Celeste's fall from the balcony was not an accident, but she had no real evidence to back up her intuition. "Do you really think it was an accident?"

"There isn't any reason to think differently."

Max looked into his green eyes, looking for a sign of doubt. He must have some of the same misgivings she did.

"Just because we have another victim who few people liked, as far as I can tell," he continued, "doesn't mean someone killed her. Now, if our last murderer wasn't behind bars, I might think a serial killer wanted to murder all of our unlikeable residents. Her husband and Peter seemed to be the only ones who were especially upset about her death."

"We never got along, but she apologized to me for how she treated me in middle school. I think she'd changed, or at least she was trying to change."

"People don't change," Detective Cruz said. "Or at least I've never seen it happen."

Was the detective that jaded? Maybe she shouldn't be surprised to hear a cop talk that way. "What about the bolt Heather picked up?"

"We couldn't get any fingerprints off it besides Heather's. And since we saw her holding it, that's to be expected."

"So, we're no closer to knowing who was at fault."

"I told you. Celeste's death has been ruled an accident." He leaned back in his chair and crossed his arms, and something about the look in his eyes made her think that he didn't agree with the ruling. He didn't say it "was an accident." He said it was "ruled an accident." Those were two different things.

Max wondered why he had come out of his way to tell her this information. Was he hoping she'd find out something so he could reopen the case? For a moment, she wondered if it were an excuse to see her but put the thought out of her mind. "So, you're not investigating any other possibilities."

"In Crystal Shores, the Mayor and Police Chief like things to be tied up neatly and as quickly as possible. You remember that they insisted on arresting Andy Fuller before we had all the evidence. They don't want people talking about a murderer running around loose in our lovely little town. I've been told to focus on other cases." The detective added with a slight smile, "Officially, there is no investigation."

Officially. Was he trying to tell her he thought it might be murder without actually saying it?

"But if I learn something that points to murder, I should let you know?" she asked.

"Definitely. You've got my cell phone number. Call me anytime."

CHAPTER 7

Keiko arrived to work shortly before eleven, dressed in a navy and white sailor suit, complete with sailor hat. Darlene scowled at her but didn't comment on her outfit. Max figured she'd given up on trying to get Keiko to dress more conservatively.

"I can't wait for Tiffany to see her wedding gown," Keiko said, brimming over with excitement. "I hope she likes it." She looked at Max with concern. "She will like it, right?"

"Of course. She's going to love it." Together, Keiko and Max had created a perfect realization of Keiko's sketch that Tiffany had fallen in love with. If anything, it looked even more impressive in real life than it did in the sketch. Max looked forward to Tiffany's reaction, too.

When Tiffany arrived, Keiko and Max took her and the dress to the dressing room and helped her into the flowing, off-the-shoulder ivory gown. The leather corset came next, and Keiko wrapped it around her. The front of the corset fastened with intricate brass hardware and the back laced up in two rows, allowing the corset to be tightened as snugly as desired.

Once Tiffany stood on the platform in the Dream Room, she looked at herself in the six mirrors with her mouth slightly opened. The gown floated around her like gossamer and the leather corset fit her like a glove. She turned around slowly, looking at the dress from all angles.

"Wow!" she finally said. "It's everything I dreamed it would be. I feel like I just stepped out of a fantasy novel."

Keiko's smile lit up her face. It was the biggest smile Max had ever seen on her.

Max checked the fitting of the dress, and suddenly Tiffany leaned over and hugged her. Then she jumped off the platform and hugged Keiko.

"I dreaded this wedding, and now I'm actually excited." She seemed to realize what she'd said and stammered, "I'm excited about getting married, but I didn't want a big wedding. I would have liked to have eloped."

Tiffany's fiancé was an accountant who wanted a traditional wedding, and Tiffany loved him enough to go through with it. Max thought that as different as they seemed, they were going to make it as a couple. They both wanted to make each other happy, which seemed like a good foundation for a marriage.

Max knew quite a lot more than the typical single

woman about marriage. She'd seen brides who were demanding, some who were controlling, and some who didn't seem to care much about their weddings, as if they were only going through the motions. She'd heard them arguing on the phone with their fiancés and being rude to their mothers. She'd become far too accurate at predicting which marriages would end in divorce, a skill she did not enjoy possessing.

But she was also quite accurate at knowing which couples would last. And when she worked with a bride who she believed had found her 'happily ever after,' it made her very happy indeed.

Max took one more look at the bride in her wedding gown from all angles. "I don't see any alterations that need to be made. I think your dress looks perfect."

"I think so, too," Tiffany said, and Keiko nodded in agreement with a blissful look on her face.

"Have you decided what you want for a headdress?" Max asked.

"Do I have to have something?" Tiffany frowned for just a moment then the blissful look returned to her face. "I think it's perfect just like this." She got an impish look on her face. "Although, I would add pointed elfin ears if I thought I could get away with it!"

"Yes!" Keiko agreed. "I would love to see you walk down the aisle in elfin ears. If I were there, I mean."

"You're going to be there, both of you. At least, you're invited. You'll come, won't you?"

"You want us at your wedding?" Max had been

invited to clients' weddings before, but it always surprised her.

"Yes, please say you'll come," Tiffany pleaded.

"Of course, we'll be there," Keiko said, speaking for both of them. "And I have an idea I want you to take a look at." She left the room and returned shortly with her sketchbook. She showed Tiffany and Max a sketch of a tiara with intricate detail. It appeared to be in brass like the corset hardware.

Tiffany stared at the drawing. "It's beautiful. But how could you get it made?"

Max asked, "Do you have metal working skills I don't know about?" There was little that would have surprised her about Keiko, a young woman with many varied talents.

"There's a local artist I've already talked to and got a quote." She told Tiffany the number. "I know it's not cheap."

"I would pay twice that. I love it!"

Keiko and Tiffany set up a time to visit the artist together. Max watched the two women talk excitedly. She loved seeing a happy bride, one who you helped make their dream wedding a reality. She couldn't imagine any other career that would bring her this much joy.

~

TIFFANY LEFT SHORTLY BEFORE NOON. MAX PACKED UP her sewing kit to take to the theater after her appointment with Eric.

Max had convinced Darlene that she needed Keiko's help at the theater. Keiko's mood improved considerably when she found out she could spend the afternoon at the theater instead of at the bridal shop with Darlene.

"I have an errand to run," Max told Darlene and Keiko, hoping they didn't ask where she was going. She didn't want to lie about going to see a possible location for her own bridal shop, but she wasn't ready to tell either of them. She wasn't even sure she was going to go ahead with the plan.

"I'm going to lunch with my mom, so I'll see you at the theater when you get there," Keiko said.

Darlene told them that Kenneth wasn't even sure they'd be going ahead with the play.

"But they have an understudy for Celeste," Keiko said.

"It's not that," Darlene said. "It's just so unseemly. Besides, what if the other actors think it's unsafe? Or worse, what if they think it's cursed?"

"Cursed?" Max raised her eyebrows. "Would they really think so?"

"Actors are a superstitious bunch, from what Kenneth has told me. Just you wait. Something will happen that they'll all interpret as a bad omen."

"I'll meet with Kenneth when I get to the theater. Until he decides if he's going to cancel the play, we'd better keep working on the costumes. I don't know if we'll be done in time if he does go through with it."

Max looked at her phone, waiting for a text from Eric. She grabbed a feather duster and absentmindedly dusted the tiaras and headpieces while she waited for him to pick her up.

She jumped when Heather burst through the door. “We need to talk,” she huffed. “I can’t wear the red velvet dress that Celeste died in. You’ll have to make another.”

Max hadn’t thought about the dress. Of course, they couldn’t use the same one. But a new one would take an entire day to recreate--extra time she hadn’t budgeted.

Keiko said, “Maybe we should wait and make sure the play’s not going to be cancelled.”

“Cancelled?” Heather cried out hysterically. “They can’t cancel the play! This is my big break.”

“Okay,” Max jumped in. “I’m sure they’re not going to cancel the play.” She had plenty of experience with hysterical brides. This wasn’t that much different. “Why don’t we take some measurements?”

Keiko waited in the showroom while Max took Heather into the dressing room and waited for her to undress to her underwear. She got her measuring tape and went to work.

“It’s pretty sad you’re getting your big break because Celeste died,” Max said.

“Yeah, it’s really tragic.” Did Max detect a note of sarcasm in her voice?

“You sound really broken up about it,” Max said, putting the measuring tape around her waist and writing down 24”. Who had a 24” waist? Had she even heard of ice cream?

“I’m not glad she’s dead, but I’m glad she’s out of my

life. That woman was a Class A bitch. And now that she's gone, I get to play Juliet. She was too old for the part, anyway. I don't know why Kenneth gave her the role."

Heather was much younger than Celeste, it was true. Max had wondered why Kenneth seemed to cater to all of Celeste's whims, including putting on *Romeo and Juliet* so she could play the lead role. Had he been enamored of her? Or did she have something on him?

She was finishing up with Heather when the text came from Eric telling her to come out front. As soon as she was done with the young actress, Max walked out the front door and climbed into his BMW.

"So, tell me about this space you found," she said.

"First, tell me about Celeste," he said, sounding indignant. "I can't believe I had to hear about it from someone else. Why didn't you call me?"

"Sorry. I was so wiped out from all the excitement last night that I didn't think of calling anyone," Max said, feeling a little guilty.

"I wish I could feel bad about it, but I don't. She spread the rumor I was gay." Max heard the hurt in his voice.

"But you are gay," Max said. Well, it was true.

"Yes, but I hadn't come out to everyone yet," he said, sounding annoyed that she didn't understand. "I wanted to let people know myself, not have them hear about it through some rumor."

"Okay, I understand. No need to get huffy with me."

"Sweetie, if I can't get huffy with you, then who can I?"

"Aw, that's the sweetest thing you've ever said to me," Max said, her voice dripping with sarcasm.

"It's true. I need friends I don't have to watch every word I say or how I say it. And for me, that's pretty much you."

"If you weren't driving, I'd hug you right now," Max said.

"Don't go getting sappy on me," Eric said and slapped her on the leg. He never was comfortable with displays of affection. It was enough that they both knew how each other felt.

Eric headed north on Coast Highway in the slow mid-day traffic. "The shop is in the center by the library, where Tom's Market is. It used to be a dress shop."

"The rent must be pricey. That's a great location."

"It's worth every penny. So, tell me about Celeste." In a fake whisper, he said, "Was it murder?"

"The police don't seem to think so. They've ruled it an accident. I'm not sure Detective Cruz agrees, though."

"You don't agree," Eric said.

Max wasn't quite sure what she thought. Her brain agreed it seemed like an accident, but her gut told her otherwise. Eric knew everyone in town even better than she did. Maybe he had an idea of who might have had it out for Celeste.

"If it was murder, who do you think did it?" she asked.

"My money is on the spouse. Although I don't care much for her husband, so I don't know how much that is coloring my opinion. You seem pretty sure it wasn't an accident."

"No," she admitted. "I think the balcony was tampered with. I don't think anyone tried to kill her. They may have been trying to hurt or scare her."

"And once again, your list of suspects is going to be a mile long."

"Why do you say that?" Max asked.

"No one liked Celeste."

"Including you?"

"Including me," he said. He pulled up to a stoplight and turned to look at her. "But I haven't been anywhere near the theater in weeks, so I'm in the clear."

"No secrets this time?" She had to be sure he was telling her the truth. As close as they were, he didn't always tell her everything. But everyone had their secrets, didn't they?

"I promise, I'm not hiding anything."

The two of them talked about everyone who was at the theater the night before and who might have a motive for murder. Twenty minutes later they hadn't made much progress coming up with a good suspect when Eric pulled into the center's parking lot. Max walked toward the empty storefront. Next door was a cupcake shop, which already had a line. There was also a yogurt shop and several women's clothing boutiques. The shop she had come to see looked narrow but deep, with tall windows framed in white wood.

A woman in a skintight, pastel blue skirt suit and high-heeled sandals sashayed toward them carrying a large tote. Her blonde hair cascaded down her shoulders in perfect spiral curls. "Eric, darling," she said sweetly. The two exchanged air kisses and told each other how amazing they both looked, until the woman finally acknowledged Max. "And you must be Max," she said, extending her hand. "I've heard so much about you. I'm Victoria."

Max shook her hand, saying, "Nice to meet you, Victoria." The real estate agent looked around thirty, but Max knew looks could be deceiving.

Victoria unlocked the front door and they walked inside. The space had honey-colored oak floors and racks for clothing along the left side of the room. A few freestanding racks remained. Max imagined a wall of wedding gowns hanging along one side and displays with tiaras, veils and other accessories. The hardwood floors were lovely, but would plush carpeting give more of a sense of luxury? The stark white walls would have to be painted a warmer color. Peach or ivory, perhaps. Would Eric agree, or would he want to do all the decorating without her input? That was another thing for them to talk about. She felt herself brimming over with excitement and full of concerns all at the same time.

She looked up and Eric and Victoria were waiting for her, so she came out of her daydream. Victoria led them back to the dressing rooms, which were small and would never work for a bridal shop. You needed a large dressing room to fit a ball gown. Behind the dressing rooms, a door led to a small office, a restroom and a storage area.

Max took special interest in the storage area, which

would also have to double as a workroom. Shelves lined one wall, and she tried to picture a worktable and sewing machine in the space. If the shelves came out, there might be room.

She had a funny feeling and noticed Eric watching her. "Why are you staring at me?" she asked him.

"I can see the wheels turning in your head," he said. "What are you thinking?"

"Do you have the measurements of this room?" Max asked Victoria.

The agent pulled a folder out of her tote and handed Max a floor plan showing the layout with all the measurements.

"Of course, we'll completely remodel, according to your specifications," Victoria said.

Max thought that sounded expensive but felt uncomfortable talking in front of a stranger. The dressing rooms would have to be completely redone, and she would need new fixtures for the showroom. It wasn't as big as Wedding Belles, but she thought she could make it work.

Eric and Max said their thanks and were noncommittal about their interest. Eric said he would be in touch, and he and Max got back into his car for the drive back to Crystal Shores.

In the car, Eric asked, "So, what do you think?"

"I love it! The location is fantastic, and with a warmer paint color, the space would be lovely. I think it needs carpet, but maybe we could leave some of the hardwood showing. The oak is beautiful."

Eric grinned. “I knew once you saw some shop spaces that you’d get excited.”

“The only thing is the storage room would have to be my workroom, and it’s a little small. I’ll have to make some sketches to see if everything would fit comfortably.” This was getting real, and she felt butterflies in her stomach. “How much is the remodeling going to cost?”

“There’s a budget for tenant improvements, as they’re called, and it’s included in the rent. You’d need to sign a three-year lease. I don’t think you need to make a lot of changes, so you should be within the budget.”

On the drive back to Crystal Shores, they talked more about the changes Max suggested. Eric told her Victoria had two other spaces for them to see before they decided.

“But the most important question of all…” he began.

“What?”

“What are you going to call your new shop?”

Max laughed happily. “I’ve been thinking of names for years, but none of them have really stuck out as ‘the one’, if you know what I mean.”

“Well, sweetie, you better start giving it some more thought, because you could be opening your own shop in just a few months.”

She felt panic coursing through her body. Why were the most exciting things that happened in your life so often the most terrifying? She took a deep breath. She could do this.

"I can't do this!" she said out loud.

Eric reached over and put his hand on hers. "Sure, you can. I'll be there every step of the way. You're an amazing, talented woman and your shop is going to be a huge success. Just take one step at a time. For today, why don't you think of names for your new shop."

"Okay." That she could do.

CHAPTER 8

Eric drove Max to the theater, while Max stared out the window at the shops of Crystal Shores. Names for her new shop bounced around in her mind. Enchantment Bridal Salon? Blushing Bridal Boutique? Or maybe she should name it after herself: Max Walters Bridal. She just didn't think her name sounded very bridal-ish. Maybe Max Bridal?

She thought about the space they'd just seen. The location was fantastic, but the more she thought about it, the more it seemed too small and cramped for a bridal salon.

"You're quiet," Eric said, interrupting her thoughts. "What's on your mind?"

"It's just not going to work," she said.

Eric slumped in the driver's seat as he pulled up to a stoplight. "I'm rushing you, aren't I? This shouldn't be about me. Why do I make everything about me?"

"Well, that's a question for another time. What I'm trying to say is that the space is too small for my shop. I was so excited I just wanted to say yes right then and there. It made me realize just how much I want to do this."

"Really?" Eric perked up and grinned at her. "I'll call Victoria when I get back and tell her to look for a bigger space."

"I need a good size workroom, and there needs to be room for a large dressing area." She was about to ask Eric's opinion on some of her ideas for names when her phone buzzed with a text from Olivia suggesting they meet for lunch. Max invited Eric to come along, but he begged off, saying he wanted to get back to his shop. He didn't trust his assistant by herself for long, but she was so likable and entertaining he couldn't bring himself to replace her.

Eric dropped her off at Rose Street Cafe, Olivia's favorite vegetarian café. Max didn't care as much about eating healthy as Olivia did, and she had been craving a French dip from Chez Mer but spending time with her friend was more important than the food. Max didn't think that way about just anyone, but Olivia was one of her favorite people.

They grabbed the last table on the tree-shaded patio and Max waited while Olivia went inside to put in their orders. She came back with two iced teas and two packets of sugar for Max.

"Darlene says Kenneth's not sure he's going ahead with the play," Max said.

"He's telling everyone that, but there's no way he's going to cancel it. He can't afford to. We need the ticket sales to keep the theater open. He'd have to refund money to everyone who's already bought tickets." Olivia shook her head thoughtfully. "No, there's no way."

"Well, I'm glad I've got Keiko to help," Max said. "There's tons of work to do. I don't know how Anastasia was going to finish it all." She also liked having the company. It kept the long hours from being too tedious.

"Anastasia didn't have a day job, though being pregnant, she may have been working slower than usual." Olivia smiled warmly. "I like having you around the theater. I wish you could be our permanent costumer."

"Darlene would never let Kenneth steal me away from her." Max emptied the packets of sugar into her tea, wondering if she should say something about her plans to open her own shop, but decided to wait until she'd made her decision. She laughed, trying not to sound awkward. "Although, the way Darlene has been acting lately, I just might accept a job offer if Kenneth made it. By the way, Heather stopped by Wedding Belles asking for a new dress to replace the one Celeste died in."

"Oh. I hadn't thought of that." Frown lines appeared for a moment in Olivia's perfect alabaster skin. "I suppose it would be gruesome to use the same dress, even if we could get it back."

"I was just thinking. Heather's coloring is so much different than Celeste's, I think a blue dress would work better for her." She'd learned a lot about what colors looked best on women working in the bridal business. Sure, most bridal gowns were white, or shades of off-white, but bridesmaids' dresses came in every shade of the rainbow. "Plus, Romeo is wearing a burgundy costume in that scene. I think the contrast would work better. Who needs to approve the change? Kenneth or the director—what was his name?"

"Ivan. I'm not sure, since Kenneth hasn't been able to get a hold of Ivan all day."

"Well, that's suspicious, especially since he never showed up last night for rehearsal." Max wondered if the director had gone missing or was just avoiding Kenneth for some reason. "What was Ivan's relationship with Celeste like?"

"I don't think Celeste liked him," Olivia said. "So, you're already asking questions, I see."

"I'm just curious. I want to figure out what really happened."

"Is Detective Cruz going to let you help out this time?"

"Like he has a choice." Max grinned slyly. "He says Celeste's death was ruled an accident, but I don't think he's completely convinced."

"What about you?"

"I don't think for a minute the bolts just came loose on their own. It's not much more than intuition, but every bone in my body is telling me someone rigged that balcony so she would fall." Max sipped at her iced tea, wondering when their food would arrive. "And then there's the psychic."

"Psychic? What psychic?"

"Apparently, Celeste had her own psychic who told

her that a nut was going to kill her, or something like that. Pretty weird, huh?"

"It doesn't surprise me that she was seeing a psychic," Olivia said. "She told me once that my aura looked dark, and she knew someone who could cleanse it for me."

"Your aura looks just fine to me. Anyway, Detective Cruz said there's no investigation, so I'll have to look into it on my own."

"Just be careful." Olivia's brow furrowed anxiously. "Remember what almost happened last time?"

"I've still got my pepper spray." Max patted her purse.

"It wasn't the pepper spray that saved you last time," Olivia reminded her.

"Well, I've still got my seam ripper," Max grinned.

A server set down a veggie burger in front of each of them. Olivia cut hers in two, and Max knew she would take half of it home with her. Max would have preferred a real burger but had to admit that this one was pretty tasty.

In between bites, Max asked more questions about Ivan. All Olivia knew was that he was an off-Broadway director who had decided to spend the summer in Crystal Shores. She thought he was originally from Russia. He didn't socialize with any of the cast, including Celeste, and didn't seem to treat her any different than any of the other actors.

After Max had finished her burger and Olivia got a box for her leftovers, Olivia took out her cell phone and called Kenneth. When she hung up the phone, she reported to Max that Kenneth agreed the blue dress would be an improvement. He also said he would take responsibility if Ivan disagreed, assuming he ever reappeared.

"Who will direct if Ivan doesn't come back?" Max wondered.

"Kenneth will take over, I'm sure. We don't have time to hire another director." Olivia grabbed her purse. "Ready to go?"

Max asked Olivia if she had time to drive her to the fabric store, and her friend agreed. Max preferred to buy her fabrics in downtown L.A., but they didn't have the time to make the long drive with so much work still to be done. The two women headed up Coast Highway a short way before turning and driving up the hill to the Sew Unique Fabric Store next to the hardware store.

While getting out of Olivia's car, Max thought she saw a tall, wiry man in the parking lot next door getting out of his truck. His shaggy brown hair and skin tanned from too much time outdoors convinced her it was Nathan, the set builder.

"I'll be right back," she told Olivia, who said she'd meet her inside the fabric store.

Max hurried over to Nathan and said hello.

"It's me, Max. Max Walters," she reminded him.

"Of course. I don't think I've seen you since you were a teenager. You were Emily's favorite babysitter."

"I heard Emily is engaged," Max said.

"Yes, to a wonderful guy. She's going to be calling

you soon so you can help her pick out a wedding dress. What brings you to the hardware store?"

"Actually, I'm shopping at the fabric store. I'm helping out with the costumes for the theater."

"The police contacted me about Celeste, asking me lots of questions," he said. He shook his head sadly. "This never should have happened."

"Yes, it seems like it was an unnecessary tragedy," Max said.

"It makes no sense that the bolts just fell out of the railing. Detective Cruz said there were several that were loose."

"Maybe someone didn't tighten them down. Don't the cast and crew help build the sets?"

"Yes, they do, but I always go back and use my power drill to tighten all the nuts. I remember doing it. They wouldn't just come loose on their own." He sounded very sure of himself.

"You couldn't have forgotten a few?" She hoped she didn't offend him by asking.

"After twenty years in construction? Not a chance. I don't even think about it—it's just automatic. Plus, I check my work after I'm done. No way were any of the nuts missing or loose." His eyes narrowed. "I know you've already helped solve one murder. Are you going to help investigate this time, too?"

"Officially, there is no murder and no investigation."

"The rumors are already spreading, and I've lost one job because of it. I think I know who's going around questioning my workmanship, but I can't prove anything. If I lose any more business, I won't be able to pay for the wedding." As an afterthought he added, "And, of course, I want whoever caused Celeste's death behind bars."

"You work for Beidleman Construction, don't you?"

"I'm one of their contractors, although their business has been slow lately. Why do you ask?" There was a touch of suspicion in his voice.

"How well do you know George Beidleman, Celeste's husband?"

"You're wondering if he killed his wife, aren't you?"

Max had to work on her subtlety. "The husband is always a suspect, don't you know that? Or don't you watch as many mysteries on TV as I do?" She attempted a laugh, but it fell flat.

"George is my boss. How well do you know your boss?" he asked. Nathan's question caught Max off guard. She'd known Darlene for more than ten years. She would surely know if she was capable of murder.

Max walked back to the fabric shop realizing Nathan hadn't actually answered her question. She found Olivia and filled her in on her conversation as they searched the aisles for the perfect blue fabric. Max had Olivia hold up a swatch of royal blue flannel while she walked to the other side of the store to get an idea of how it would look from the audience. Flannel was a wonderful substitute for velvet, and you could hardly tell the difference from a distance. As an added benefit, it was cheaper and easier to work with. The fabric would be perfect, and after picking out matching thread and a zipper, they were on their way to the theater.

~

WITH KEIKO'S HELP, MAX ADJUSTED THE PATTERN SHE found for Juliet's dress so it would fit Heather, and Keiko helped her cut out the blue fabric. While Max sewed the new dress, Keiko researched a coif online.

"It's just a cap," Keiko said, "with straps to hold it in place. Do we have any white linen?"

"No idea," Max admitted, and the two women spent the next twenty minutes digging through pieces of fabric left over from countless plays that had been performed over the years.

"Will this work?" Max said, holding up a swatch of off-white cotton fabric.

"I'll make it work," Keiko said, and in less than an hour, she had created a coif. With that done, she helped Max with the blue gown, pinning pieces together for her to sew, which helped speed up the process.

"You know what's been bothering me?" Max said. "The night Celeste died, she told me that a psychic had told her a nut was out to get her or kill her. I wish I could remember exactly what she said."

"A nut?" Keiko's eyes got wide. "Doesn't a nut hold a bolt in place? That's very interesting. Do you think the psychic could really tell the future?"

"I don't believe in psychics." Max was far too practical for that, although she knew there were things in life that couldn't be explained. "It's just a really odd coincidence, don't you think?"

"I think it's more than odd. I think it's eerie. What was the psychic's name? Did she tell you?"

"Yes. It was Madam something. Gina or Jana. I'm not sure."

"I'll look her up." Keiko said, happily jumping up from her seat to head for her computer.

"No, you won't. You're going to keep sewing." Max could get lots of work out of Keiko, but only if she could keep her away from the computer. What was it with these young people? She laughed to herself. She was starting to sound like her dad.

A little before six, they could hear the actors begin to file into the theater for rehearsal. Max stopped sewing and crept into the hallway to see what she could overhear. As she suspected, most of the talk was about Celeste and the rumors were flying. One actor said she was pregnant, and another said she was getting a divorce. Two men who played smaller roles started to argue. Max only heard part of their conversation, but she did pick out Celeste's name.

Fiona appeared, startling her. She was holding a black cat.

"What are you up to, lurking backstage?" Fiona asked. "Listening for clues?"

"Yes, but all I've heard is crazy rumors," Max said. "What is Josie doing here?" The cat, which spent her days at the yarn shop, didn't look particularly happy.

"Simon is visiting Teresa in Canada, so I'm watching Josie," Fiona said. Josie was their neighbor

Simon's cat, and Fiona's sister Teresa had fallen in love with the cat when she found it last spring. Then she fell in love with Simon, Josie's owner.

"Kenneth said we had a mouse problem, so I volunteered Josie. I don't know if she's caught a mouse in her life, but I figured she'd be happier here than at home alone. She prefers to be around people."

"She can stay in the costume shop with us if you want," Max said. She wasn't sure if Josie liked her (the cat was very particular about people), but she liked the cat and hoped Josie would warm up to her.

Fiona and Max joined Keiko in the costume shop. Fiona replaced her baseball cap with the coif that Keiko had made and looked like she'd gone back in time.

"It's perfect," Fiona said, and Max and Keiko agreed. "I'd better get moving. Tonight's a tech rehearsal, so it may run late. Just bring Josie out to me if you're ready to leave before we're done."

"Fiona," Max said, hesitating, "would you mind keeping your ears open and let me know if you hear anything?"

"You can count on me," she said and left the room.

Josie strolled around the costume shop, and after investigating everything to her satisfaction, walked back to Max. She jumped onto Max's lap, curled up and fell asleep, purring loudly.

Max smiled. "Looks like she's finally gotten used to me." She realized she was pinned to the spot by the sleeping cat. "I guess I'm not moving anytime soon," she told Keiko. "Would you hand me those pieces?"

The whirring sound of the two sewing machines

filled the small room while Max sewed the blue dress and Keiko worked on one of Brian's costumes. He had three costume changes during the play, and each of the costumes was very intricate. Max wished Anastasia had designed simpler costumes. Most of the details couldn't be seen from the audience anyway, so Max eliminated any of them she could.

Max was startled to see an elderly woman inside the doorway shakily holding a tray with teacups. The sound of her footsteps had been drowned out by the noise of the sewing machines. Max motioned to Keiko to stop sewing so she could hear the woman.

With a creaky voice, she repeated, "I brought you tea."

Max wanted to say, "who are you?" but instead she said, "Why, thank you," clearing off space on the table for the tray.

"I brought you Darjeeling," the woman said in barely more than a whisper. She lifted the teacup and saucer, which trembled in her hands. Max jumped up, knocking Josie on the floor, and quickly took the cup from the old woman. The cat gave her a dirty look and walked over to the sofa. Olivia must have told the woman that her favorite tea was Darjeeling.

"Sorry, Josie," Max said.

"I like it with sugar and cream, don't you?" the woman asked.

Max nodded. A pitcher of cream and a sugar bowl were on the tray.

"And for you, young lady," she said to Keiko, "I brought green tea. I hope that's all right."

"Of course," Keiko said, "I love green tea," and hurried over to take the teacup from her.

"I also brought you a plate of my homemade cinnamon cookies." She placed the plate of cookies on the table along with the cream and sugar and picked up the empty tray. "I won't keep you from your work. Have a lovely evening, girls." She slowly shuffled out the door.

Max and Keiko looked at each other. "Who was that?" they both said at the same time.

"I don't know," Max answered, "but I like her already. She brought us tea and cookies. Olivia must have sent her in and told her what our favorite teas are. That was really sweet of her." Max added cream and sugar to her tea and then reached for a cookie. She took a bite and grimaced. She grabbed a napkin and spit the cookie out.

"That bad?" Keiko asked.

"You try it," Max suggested.

"No way! Not after the reaction you had."

"I think she used a whole jar of cinnamon." Max stared at the cookies, disappointed. Now she really wanted cookies.

Keiko took a sip of her tea. "At least the tea is good. It is delicious, actually."

"Yes, mine is wonderful. We'll have to get rid of the cookies before she comes back so we don't hurt her feelings."

Max and Keiko sat drinking tea and enjoying their break. Josie seemed to forgive Max and hopped back on her lap and went back to sleep.

"I ran into Nathan when we went to the fabric shop," Max said.

"What was Nathan doing at the fabric shop?" Keiko asked.

"He was going to the hardware store next door. I saw him in the parking lot. He seemed very sure he tightened down all the nuts, which reminds me. Not only did two bolts come loose, but there must be two nuts around here somewhere, too." Max was lost in thought. "The fact that they've only found one bolt seems a bit suspicious to me."

"So, it sounds like it wasn't an accident to me, don't you think?" Keiko asked.

"If Nathan's being truthful, then I have to agree."

It was nearly ten o'clock when Fiona came back in the costume shop to retrieve Josie.

"Fiona," Max asked, "who is the little old lady who brought us tea?"

"Who are you talking about?" Fiona asked. "I'm the only little old lady around here."

CHAPTER 9

Max knew that Darlene couldn't do without her and Keiko at the bridal shop on a Saturday. The costumes at the theater would just have to wait until later. Shortly after Darlene unlocked the front door, Susan Brown came in for her last fitting, glowing just like when she first told Max about being engaged.

The day flew by with several more appointments and a few drop-ins, as usual. Max found the perfect dress for three different brides, all of whose mothers were in tears, seeing their daughters in bridal gowns. Keiko ran up and down the stairs several times, retrieving gowns in other sizes and hung back up at least a dozen dresses after the clients left.

No sewing got done on Saturdays, generally, and Max was happy to get a break from being hunched over a sewing machine, at least for a few hours.

At three, Darlene announced that she could get by without them for the rest of the day.

"I'm beat," Max told Keiko as they got into Keiko's car. "I'll be happy to sit down and sew for a few hours, although I really feel like sitting in front of the TV for the rest of the day."

"You didn't have to run up and down the stairs ten times like I did," Keiko said. "And I have Aikido class tonight." She pulled into the theater parking lot. "I'll help out for a few hours until it's time to go."

"That's right. I forgot you have class on Saturdays," Max said as they entered the theater. "How's it coming? Are you able to kill someone with your bare hands yet?"

Keiko rolled her eyes like a petulant teenager, which made Max laugh. "That's not what Aikido is about."

"Okay, can you defend yourself if someone tries to attack you?"

"Oh, yes. I can kick some butt. There is no need to worry about me."

"Maybe I should take some classes when we're done with these costumes." Max thought it would be smart to be able to protect herself, especially considering the way this year had been going so far.

Keiko clapped her hands happily. "I would love to take you with me. I will arrange for you to have a trial class. I think you will like it. I find it very relaxing."

"Really? I definitely should try it then." She opened the costume shop door and sighed at the sight of fabric and costumes everywhere. "I think the first thing I need to do is straighten up."

"It looks worse than it is," Keiko reassured her,

hanging up costumes. "We must have been really tired when we left last night."

Was the room in this much disarray when they left it last night? Max saw Anastasia's costume journal laying on the table where she left it but couldn't help but think something was missing. Where was her notebook? She asked Keiko if she'd seen it. They scoured the room, but it didn't turn up.

"Maybe I took it home with me," Max said, giving up on the search. Did someone take it? Who knew she kept notes of all the evidence and suspects? Pretty much everyone, she had to admit to herself.

A loud knock interrupted her thoughts. Max opened the door and let Kenneth in. Funny how the person who ran the theater was the only one who didn't burst into the room unannounced.

After a cursory greeting, he got to the point. "The shoes just arrived, and they're all wrong. They sent us pilgrim shoes! Can you imagine? I suppose some theater performing The Crucible got all of our Renaissance footwear. I called the supplier, and it will take weeks to get us the right shoes."

Max didn't know where they could get new shoes in such a short period of time.

"We can make shoes," Keiko said. Max looked at her dubiously.

"Really? How are hand-sewn shoes going to look?" He paused, thinking it over. "What am I saying? It's not like we have a choice. Do it!"

Max asked Keiko, "Are you sure about this?" Keiko

had a sheepish look on her face, apparently realizing she had just volunteered them for even more work.

"Pretty sure?" Keiko said, not sounding convincing. "Send the actors in one at a time so we can trace their feet. I remember seeing some large pieces of faux leather. If there's not enough, I can run to the fabric shop tomorrow."

Max suddenly felt like she had been cast in an episode of Project Runway with limited resources and a nearly impossible deadline. At least she didn't have to make a costume out of items only bought at a grocery store.

Rehearsals started earlier today, and Fiona arrived around four o'clock, bringing Josie with her. Josie seemed a bit miffed that Max wouldn't sit down so she could snuggle on her lap. Instead, Josie found a pile of fabric on the sofa and curled up on it.

"So, what's this about shoes?" Fiona asked.

Max explained about the mix up and the solution Keiko had come up with. She had Fiona stand on a piece of brown Kraft paper so she could trace her feet.

"So, how's the investigation going?" Fiona asked. "Is Detective Cruz going to accept your help?"

"It turns out there is no murder investigation, but of course they'll want to find out who was at fault." Max told Fiona what the detective had told her.

"Well, let me tell you what I overheard," Fiona said with a gleam in her eye.

Max's interest was certainly piqued. "Spill," she said.

"Apparently, Ivan and Celeste had a huge argument

the night before she died. Most of the actors had left, but Zach overheard them."

"Zach?" Max asked.

"He's playing Tybalt. Anyway, Celeste was insisting that he fire Heather and he refused. She said she was going to go to Kenneth."

Max remembered Celeste telling her that the actor who played Tybalt was always lurking about. "Why did their argument get so heated?"

"Ivan is very temperamental," Fiona said. "He's had blow ups with several actors. Quite the temper, that one."

"Interesting." Max wondered if he had enough of a temper that he would loosen the bolts on the railing, hoping she would fall and be injured. It was suspicious that he wasn't there the night she fell and hadn't been seen since. "You know, before Jennifer was murdered, this was a nice quiet town. The biggest crimes were probably jaywalking and people walking their dogs without a leash."

"I can't believe we have another murder so soon. Or ever," Fiona said.

"It could have been an accident." Max had to admit it was a possibility. Investigating a murder added some excitement to her otherwise fairly uneventful life. Was that leading her to see murder where there was none?

Fiona put her hands on her hips. "I know you, and I can tell just by looking at you that you don't believe that. At least you'll find out who's to blame even if that Detective Cruz isn't doing anything to help."

"I wouldn't say that," Max said. She wasn't sure why

she felt the need to defend the detective, but she didn't like Fiona criticizing him. "I have a feeling he's doing his own unofficial investigating. It's just going to be harder for him, that's all. And that's where I come in. Hopefully, I can learn enough to allow him to reopen the case."

Brian knocked on the door and entered. "Kenneth sent me."

Fiona said she'd leave them alone, winking at her as she left the room. Was Fiona trying to fix them up? Max had him stand on a piece of brown paper to measure his feet.

"So, how have you been since high school, Max?"

While she traced his feet on the paper, Max told him about design school and her move to New York where she worked as a pattern maker until her mother fell ill. Brian expressed his condolences for the loss of her mother ten months ago.

"You know, I always had a crush on you in high school," he admitted.

"Me?" Max said, honestly surprised. He'd never shown any sign of it. She measured across the top of his foot, wrote down the number, and stood up.

"You were such a cute nerd with your braces and ponytails. You helped me pass chemistry, you know. But I didn't think you'd go out with me, and I was too shy to ask anyway. I didn't have much self-esteem back then."

"I didn't date much in high school," Max said. "I was pretty shy, too." When she said she didn't date much, she really meant not at all. She wouldn't even have gone to the prom if her mom hadn't convinced Eric to take her. She dated a little after high school, but she always held out hope for one person. Andy was her childhood sweetheart, or at least she thought he was, until years later when she found out he didn't feel the same about her. After a bad relationship with a man who cheated on her, she decided to wait until the right man came along. She hoped she wouldn't be waiting too long.

"Then you joined speech club and started winning all those competitions," he said.

"Yeah, my mom made me join." Max remembered arguing with her mom and ultimately losing. "It did a lot for my confidence, but nothing for my popularity. It made me more of a nerd as far as everyone in school was concerned."

"How about we go out for dinner? We can talk about old times and catch up. I don't have to be at rehearsal on Monday. Whatcha say?"

Before she knew it, Max had agreed. She felt a flutter inside. Was this a date? Or just old friends getting together to catch up?

"Do you still live behind your dad's house on Rose Street?" he asked.

Max nodded, wondering how he knew where she lived. It didn't really surprise her, though. In this small of a town, most of the residents probably knew her dad lived in the storybook looking house and that she lived over the garage.

Someone knocked on the door, and Max was disappointed to be interrupted. She called out, "Come in."

Detective Cruz entered the room and looked at both of them, saying nothing.

"I'll pick you up at seven," Brian said, gave her a kiss on the cheek, and left.

"What can I do for you Detective?' Max felt her face flush. The kiss had been unexpected and left her feeling flustered, especially since it had happened in front of Detective Cruz.

"How well do you know Brian Lovett?"

That wasn't what she expected him to say. "I've known him since high school. Don't tell me he's one of your suspects?" Max was ready to give him a list of all the reasons he couldn't be guilty.

"Of course not," he said, pulling out a chair and sitting down. "There's no murder investigation, so there aren't any suspects."

"So, you haven't narrowed it down, either." Max could tell by the look on his face that she was on the right track. "I haven't had much time to even think about the case." She took the paper with Brian's footprints traced on it to the table and started cutting it out.

"You know, it's pretty much everyone's opinion that Brian was having an affair with Celeste."

Max explained that he put up with her advances because he wanted to get his Equity card. "You can't believe every rumor you hear, detective, surely you know that."

"I don't trust him," he said. "Are you going out with him?"

"Is that any of your business?" she asked, and then,

seeing the hurt look on his face, said, "We're having dinner Monday." What did he have against Brian? If she didn't know better, she would think he was jealous. But that would mean that the detective was interested in her. "Why don't you trust him?"

"It's just a feeling I have. I don't want to see you getting hurt."

"I really appreciate your concern, but I can take care of myself," Max said firmly, although she was surprised to realize she liked him worrying about her.

"Gee," Detective Cruz said, leaning back in the chair and crossing his arms. "Where have I heard that before?"

"Hey!" She knew he was talking about when a murderer had held her at gunpoint. "I took care of myself pretty well, if you ask me."

"Let's just try to keep you out of trouble this time. I'm going to be keeping an eye on you." He cleared his throat. "You know, just to make sure you're safe."

CHAPTER 10

Max rather liked the idea of Detective Cruz keeping an eye on her, even if she wanted to protest that she didn't need babysitting. "Well, the best way to keep everybody safe is to find out who killed Celeste. I mean, if it turns out it wasn't an accident. I was thinking." She pulled over another chair and sat across from him. She whispered, even though there was no one else in the room to hear her. "Like you said, everyone thought Brian and Celeste were having an affair. I wonder if her husband thought so, too."

Detective Cruz leaned forward. "I interviewed him before her death was ruled an accident, and if he had any suspicions, he didn't let on. Besides, how could he have gotten up on the balcony without anyone noticing him?"

"The theater is pretty much empty all day." He was so close, she caught a whiff of his scent. He smelled fresh and clean, like he had just taken a shower. The thought of him in the shower that popped into her head made her feel awkward, so she stood up and busied herself with the patterns for the shoes. "Kenneth and Olivia are the only ones around and they mostly stay in their offices. Anyone could have unscrewed those bolts." But whatever happened to the other bolt and the nuts? "Did you ever find the rest of the missing hardware?"

"We didn't see anything else the night of the murder when we were looking for the missing bolts. Either they weren't tightened down in the first place, or someone loosened them. If that's the case, we don't even know when it happened." Detective Cruz saw the plate of cookies on the table and before Max could stop him, he had snatched one up and taken a bite. "Mmm... these taste homemade. Did you make them?"

Was he kidding? Those cookies were inedible. "No, a little old lady brought us tea and cookies last night, but I don't know who she is."

"I'm sorry. That was rude of me to take one of your cookies without asking. I haven't eaten since breakfast."

"That's okay. You can take the rest of the cookies with you if you like."

"Really? Thanks!" He happily wrapped the remaining cookies in a napkin and put them in his pocket.

After the detective left, Max realized she didn't know why he stopped by. Was he hoping to find out what she'd learned? Perhaps he'd only wanted to warn her, which indicated he didn't think it was an accident.

She got to work cutting out fabric for the shoes and

was interrupted several times by actors that Kenneth sent in to have their feet traced.

Keiko arrived just before eight with sushi. Max hadn't realized how hungry she was until she saw the food. Keiko told her about her Aikido class while they ate. Every so often, she stood up and demonstrated a move. Max was impressed.

"Get up and I'll show you how to flip someone," Keiko said.

Max didn't move. "No way." Keiko tried to convince her, but Max refused stubbornly. "I hope I don't have to flip someone at my first class."

Keiko laughed. "No, it's an advanced move. I wasn't going to actually flip you."

"That's okay. I'll take your word for it. Unless we get another volunteer who's more easily persuaded."

When they finished eating, Max showed her how to cut out the fabric for the shoes and explained how they went together. Keiko got to work on them while Max sewed the blue dress.

"So, Brian's taking me to dinner on Monday," Max said casually.

Keiko squealed. "A date! That is great news."

"I thought you didn't like Brian," Max said.

"That's just because of all the rumors. I have learned that theater people really like to gossip and half of what they say is lies."

"Is that so."

"Besides," Keiko continued. It's about time you went on a date."

"What do you mean, it's about time? It hasn't been that long."

Keiko shook her head. "It has been a while. You haven't gone out since—"

A knock on the door interrupted Keiko's thought and kept Max from grilling Keiko about her love life. Eric entered before she could call out, "come in."

"Eric!" Max said gleefully, jumping up from the sewing machine to give him a hug. "What are you doing here? Have you found another--" She stopped herself just in time before she said too much.

"Another what?" Keiko asked, looking up from the fabric pieces she was pinning together. "Ouch! I just poked myself with a pin." She stared at her finger to see if she'd drawn blood.

Max grimaced. Why had she said that? She shook her head at Eric, hoping he wouldn't say anything in front of Keiko. She wasn't ready to talk about opening her own shop yet. If she did, she would love to have Keiko come work for her. But Keiko was terrible at keeping secrets, and Max definitely wasn't ready for Darlene to know what she was up to. Eric took the hint and didn't mention anything about her opening her own bridal shop.

"No, I haven't found another location for a second flower shop, but I do have one I'd like to take you to see with me on Sunday. But that's not why I'm here. Kenneth called me today and begged me to fill in and play Mercutio. One of the actors had to drop out at the last minute. Kenneth called me in a panic and pleaded with me to fill in."

"That's awesome!" Max said. She'd never seen Eric perform before and looked forward to seeing him on the stage.

"I wasn't going to do it, but I found out there would be sword fighting involved. That sold me. I rarely get to use my fencing skills these days."

"Fencing skills?" She was always learning something new about her friends.

"Yes, I learned in college. I'm sure I told you before, didn't I? Anyway, Kenneth sent me in," he said. "Something about shoes."

While Keiko traced his feet, Max asked about his new boyfriend, Jonathan.

"He took me to the driving range today," he said.

"You're getting serious about this whole golfing thing," Max said with surprise. "I thought you hated golf." He almost didn't go out with Jonathan a second time because he was a golfer. Apparently, he'd overcome his aversion to the game.

"I hated the idea of golf, but I actually had a good time. Jonathan is a very good teacher. Now we just need to work on your love life."

"She has a date!" Keiko blurted out.

Max glared at Keiko halfheartedly, but Keiko just shrugged. Max felt her cheeks redden.

"Keiko can flip you," Max said. "Do you want her to show you?"

Eric gave Keiko a worried look. "No, that's okay. Nice way to try and change the subject. So, what about this date of yours?"

"Well, I don't know if it's really a date. We're going out to dinner on Monday."

"Who's this maybe date with?" Eric asked.

"Brian." When Max saw his blank look, she continued, "Brian Lovett. I went to high school with him. He's playing Romeo."

"Oh, I know who you're talking about." He gave her a sly grin. "He's very handsome."

"Well, I suppose so," she said, although she agreed completely. She even thought he was cute in high school, but he was really good looking now.

"I'll look forward to hearing on Tuesday morning how the date went," Eric said. "Stop by my shop on your way to work and fill me in on all the details." He hugged her and turned to go when she stopped him.

"Wait, what about your costume?" She hoped he was the same size as the actor who was originally set to play Mercutio. She went over to the rack and grabbed the costume. "Try this on. I hope we don't need to make you a new costume. I might just lose it."

"You? Lose it? That's something I've never seen." He took the costume and went into the closet they called a dressing room.

"It takes a lot to make me lose it," she called out through the door. "But it's not a pretty sight when it happens, I can tell you that much." Very few people had seen her have a meltdown. She tried to stay in control no matter how crazy things got. She had practice from working at Wedding Belles where things could get extremely hectic, especially on a Saturday like today. Plus, her job in New York was high pressure, with one deadline after another and demanding bosses not unlike Darlene.

Eric stepped out of the dressing room, and Max scowled. The costume was too big, but that was much better than being too small. It was much easier to take in a costume than to let it out. By the time she was done with him, Eric looked like a pincushion.

"Okay, you can take it off, but be careful you don't poke yourself with all the pins," she warned.

"Yes, it hurts," Keiko said. "Trust me."

Max unzipped the costume for him, and Eric went back into the dressing room and came out uninjured. "Make me look good, sweetie. I want all eyes on me, not on your new boyfriend."

Max slugged him in the arm.

Heather was one of the last actors to come into the costume shop to have her feet traced for the shoes Max and Keiko would be making.

“Hast thou finished my gown?” Heather asked.

Max hadn’t spent a lot of time around actors, but she knew they could be eccentric. Apparently, Heather was staying in character. Max showed her the blue dress which still had a lot of work to be done but was coming along nicely.

“I never would have slain her,” Heather said, although Max hadn’t asked the question.

“Why do you say that?”

“Because I’m Juliet, so it would be like killing myself.”

Max decided not to point out that Juliet did actually kill herself in the play.

"It's because Celeste said the name of the Scottish Play," Heather continued. "I heard her say that when she was older, she was looking forward to playing Lady M."

Max looked at Keiko, who shrugged.

"Lady M?" Max asked.

"You never say the name when you're in a theater. It's bad luck. Everyone knows that!" She seemed to think they should know what she meant.

"I still don't know what play we're talking about," Max said, confused.

"You know. Out, out damn spot!" she said very dramatically.

"Oh…" Max began.

"Don't say it!" Heather nearly shouted. "Or you'll be the next one to die."

Keiko said, "I don't believe in superstitions. I also am not familiar with Shakespeare's plays, so there's not much danger of me saying the name of one of them. Unless it's *Midsummer Night's Dream.* It's not *Midsummer Night's Dream,* is it?"

"No, of course not. Celeste was already old enough to play Lady You-Know-Who. I don't know who she was kidding. And she was way too old to play Juliet. I was born to play Juliet, and the timing is perfect because I'm only nineteen. 'Tis a shame she had to die, but you know what they say. Things happen for a reason."

"Wasn't Juliet only fourteen?"

"Well, you're not going to find a fourteen-year-old

to play the role," Heather snapped. "She'd have to be home in bed by the end of the second act."

Max wondered if Heather were implying that Celeste died so that she could play Juliet. How badly did Heather want the part? Enough to kill?

CHAPTER 11

Max walked onto the stage looking for Peter, since he was the only actor who hadn't had his feet traced for shoes. Peter was nowhere to be found, but she saw Detective Cruz walking up the center aisle of the auditorium. What was he doing back here?

"May I speak to you, Kenneth?" he asked. Kenneth walked down the steps from the stage and met the detective in front of the first row.

Max did her best to look inconspicuous while trying to overhear the conversation that Cruz was having with Kenneth. She heard him ask about Ivan's whereabouts. The director hadn't been seen since Celeste's death, but why was Cruz looking for him if the case was closed?

"The address he gave you is a mailbox from The Postal Center," Cruz said. Everyone on stage had stopped what they were doing, and they were all listening to the conversation. "All the information you gave me appears to be fake. The real Ivan Petrov is an off-Broadway director who lives in New York and hasn't been near Crystal Shores. Do you have any additional information on this imposter?"

Kenneth admitted something seemed suspicious about a New York director wanting to do community theater, but Ivan had told him he needed a break from the Manhattan summer and wanted to get back to his roots.

"But I called the last theaters he worked for, and they vouched for him," Kenneth said. "Although, neither mentioned how temperamental he could be. He flew off the handle at the slightest provocation."

"I called the numbers you gave me, and they're disconnected," Cruz said. "Turns out they were burner phones."

"I knew there was something fishy about that man," Kenneth said. "But I needed a director, and John Story recommended him. He's a director I used to work with who lives in New York now."

"Did you actually talk to your director friend?" Cruz asked. "Because I did, and he said he doesn't know Ivan, and he hasn't talked to you recently."

"No, he emailed me," Kenneth said, frowning. "He said Ivan was moving to the west coast and he recommended him highly. I can't believe I was that gullible."

"I suppose Ivan's long gone by now, whatever his real name is. Do you have any pictures of him?"

"He made an excuse the day we had publicity shots taken. I didn't think anything of it at the time." Kenneth turned to the stage. He and Detective Cruz became aware that every actor was staring at them.

"Anyone catch Ivan in a picture?" Kenneth asked in his loud stage voice and turned back to Cruz. "These young people are always taking selfies, even though I ask them not to bring their phones on stage during rehearsals."

Every actor pulled their phones out and started looking at their pictures. Heather spoke up first.

"Here's one," she announced, and walked to the edge of the stage handing Kenneth her phone.

Kenneth showed the picture to Cruz. There was Heather in a low-cut top making a duck face, and clear as day, Ivan stood in the background.

The detective handed back the phone to Heather with his card. "Email that picture to me right now," he ordered. Max watched the detective walk back down the aisle until she saw the front door close behind him. Did he think Ivan had something to do with Celeste's death? She couldn't imagine what the motive might be, but maybe Detective Cruz knew something she didn't. It was certainly suspicious that he had disappeared into thin air.

Fiona told Max that Peter had the day off from rehearsal, since he was bartending at the Quick Fox. He had someone to cover for him once the show opened but wasn't able to get anyone to work for him tonight. Olivia was standing in for him in the few scenes he was in so they could check the lighting.

Max sent Keiko home just after ten and told her she didn't have to come to the theater the next day, but

Keiko insisted. Since they'd been working so many hours, they agreed they would take the morning off and come to the theater around noon. After Keiko left, Max lay down on the sofa to rest her eyes for a moment and fell fast asleep. She dreamed that she couldn't breathe, and someone was holding her down. Then Keiko was swatting her face with fur mittens on. She opened her eyes and Josie was sitting on her chest staring at her with a paw raised ready to give her another swat.

"All right, I'll get up." She looked at the clock and told Josie, "You only let me sleep for fifteen minutes." She sighed. "I guess that's just as well. I have a lot to get done. Do you mind?" she asked when Josie didn't move. The cat leapt off her chest and Max stood and stretched just as Fiona came into the room.

"That cat is a good alarm clock," Max said.

Fiona laughed. "Don't I know it? I haven't slept past six since she's been staying with me. How late are you working, anyway?"

"Maybe another hour. I want to make some more progress on Heather's blue dress."

"Well, I'm done for the night, so I'll see you tomorrow. Or I should say, we'll see you tomorrow." Fiona scooped up Josie and said goodnight.

Max turned up the radio to try to help her stay alert. She was bent over the worktable, pinning the blue dress when she sensed someone behind her. She twirled around in a panic only to find the little old lady from the night before. Max turned the radio down so she could hear what she said.

"I brought you chamomile tea tonight. It's so late, I didn't think you'd want anything with caffeine. Besides," she continued, "chamomile is so relaxing, and you look a little tense."

Sure, from people sneaking up on her. "That's very thoughtful," Max said. "I didn't get your name. I'm Max."

"Oh, everyone knows who you are. I'm Evelyn. I made you snickerdoodles."

Max stared at the old woman. "Do I know you?"

"No, of course not," the woman laughed, putting down the tray. "Now, don't you work too late, honey. You need your mind sharp. You've got a lot to figure out, the sooner the better."

"What do I have to figure out?" Did Evelyn know she was looking for a murderer? "Do you know anything?"

"I know you have a lot of costumes to finish. But you'll get done in time. I have complete confidence in you."

Evelyn turned and shuffled slowly out of the room and down the hall. Max sipped the tea but skipped the cookies. She didn't want to take any chances that they were as bad as the last ones.

Max went down the hall and knocked on Olivia's door. She was really curious who Evelyn was, but she kept getting away before she figured out how to ask her what she was doing there without sounding rude. Olivia wasn't in her office, so Max made a mental note to ask her later.

Max realized it seemed really quiet. Was anyone

still there? Her footsteps echoed in the silence, and when she got to the stage, it was empty. Had everyone left and not said anything? She hoped her dad was still up and willing to give her a ride. The auditorium seemed eerie with no one around. A shiver crawled up her spine.

A shrill cry rang out and Max didn't have time to react before Heather came running out from behind the curtains.

"I saw her! I saw her!" Heather said in a panic.

"Saw who?" Max asked.

"Celeste!"

"What are you talking about?" Max asked, confused.

"I saw her ghost!"

CHAPTER 12

"Call 911!" Heather was in near hysterics.

"Because you saw a ghost?" Max could just imagine the dispatcher's reaction. She wasn't about to make that call. "Breathe, Heather."

Heather took a deep breath and then stated firmly, "I really did see her." At least she sounded calmer.

"Why don't you tell me what you saw? I'm sure there's an explanation." Max looked around the stage and found an ornate chair off to the side. She led Heather to it and had her sit down.

"The explanation is that I saw Celeste's ghost!" Heather insisted.

Max was afraid Heather was going to get worked up again. "Let me get you some water." She started to leave the stage.

"No!" Heather insisted, standing up again and grabbing Max by the arm. "Don't leave me. I never want to be alone in this theater again."

They both jumped when one of the outer doors of

the theater slammed. Max's heart beat wildly while she stared at the front of the auditorium until moments later the inner door opened and Richard appeared.

"Dad!" Max called out. She didn't believe in ghosts, but she was glad to see him.

"I've been trying to call you, but you're not answering your phone," he scolded.

"Really? I didn't hear it ring." She really needed to program a louder ringer on her phone. She must not have heard it over the music. "I'm glad to see you. Heather thinks she just saw a ghost."

Heather folded her arms across her face and huffed, "I did see a ghost. Celeste's ghost."

"Interesting," Richard said. "What did she look like?"

"What?" The question caught Heather off guard. "I don't know. I didn't see her that clearly. I was behind the theater having a smoke when I saw a woman in the mist."

Richard and Max looked at each other, and Max was sure they were having the same thought. Heather had a very active imagination.

"What are you doing here so late?" Max asked Heather. "And where is everyone else?"

"Oh, they must have just left while I was outside. Maybe they thought I'd already left. Would you walk me to my car?" Heather asked Richard, who agreed gallantly. Heather looped her hand through his arm, and they headed for the side door that led to the parking lot. Heather called out to Max, "I'm not coming back until they perform an exorcism on this place."

Max wondered how Kenneth was going to take that news. He no longer had an understudy for Juliet, so he needed her if they were going to perform the play. Well, it wasn't her problem, thank goodness.

"Ready to go home?" Max asked her father when he reappeared.

"I'm ready if you are," he said.

"I am so ready. It was a really long day today, and there's still so much to do. Keiko and I are coming in late tomorrow. Do you have plans for breakfast?" she asked.

"Nope." They walked outside and headed toward Richard's car. "We haven't gone to brunch for a while. How about the Beachcomber?"

"Really?" It was one of her favorite places for brunch. It had also been one of her mother's favorites, and Max suspected that was why he hadn't taken her there lately. "Are you buying?"

"Of course. I wouldn't have it any other way."

Richard was very generous, especially to his only daughter, and always treated unless she insisted on paying, which she did occasionally, just to remind him that she was a grown up. "That sounds wonderful."

When Max got to her apartment, she threw on her pajamas, brushed her teeth, and crawled into bed, without taking off her makeup.

CHAPTER 13

In her dream, there was a pounding on the costume shop door. She'd locked the door to stay safe from the murderer. Then she remembered that the costume shop door didn't have a lock. She looked around for a weapon, but all she found was a pair of scissors. She woke up then, realizing the pounding was on her front door. When she looked through the glass panes, she found her dad looking relieved to see her. She opened the door to let him in.

"It's nine o'clock. Were you going to sleep all day? And don't you ever answer your phone?" he asked. Her dad was a total sweetheart except when he hadn't eaten. She knew his grumpiness would go away as soon as he had breakfast.

"I must have forgotten to plug it in when I got home." She didn't think nine was that late to sleep after you worked a fourteen-hour day. There seemed to be some sort of conspiracy to keep her from sleeping in late.

"I'm thinking of getting you a landline. You're always forgetting to plug that thing in. Get dressed," he ordered. "I'm hungry!"

She went back into the bedroom, and he called after her, "And plug in that phone!"

Her dad didn't sound like he was willing to wait for her to fix her hair and put on makeup, so a ponytail would have to do for today. She threw on jeans, a black t-shirt, and sneakers. It felt nice to be casual for a change. A quick look in the mirror reminded her she hadn't taken her makeup off the night before. She took a washcloth and wiped the raccoon eyes away and washed her face. Grabbing a hoodie and her purse, they were off to The Beachcomber.

Richard drove his Mini Cooper south along Coast Highway, as she absentmindedly watched all the shops and restaurants of Crystal Shores they passed by.

"Pull over!" she cried out.

Richard pulled his car to the side of the road. "What is it? Is everything okay?" he asked.

"What? Oh, yes, everything's fine. Sorry about that. I just saw a shop for rent."

Max confided in her father the offer Eric had made her to open her own bridal shop. Richard was appropriately encouraging and concerned, telling her what a great idea it was and making sure she had thought everything through. Max knew her father wanted the best for her but would never stop worrying about her no matter how old she got.

They got out of the car and walked a block or so back up Coast Highway until they stood in front of a large retail space. The front door stood open, so they walked inside.

Two workmen were removing fixtures from the walls, and when Max asked if they could look around, they didn't object. The front room was wide and expansive. Toward the back, a door led to a large open area with a restroom to one side and a small kitchenette. Max could envision how it could be separated into a large workroom and a dressing area. At the rear were stairs, so she climbed up to a huge storage area, much like they had at Wedding Belles.

"Dad, it's perfect," Max said.

"Do you think so?" he said.

"There's just one problem. It's in Crystal Shores." Her shoulders slumped. "This little town can't support two bridal shops, and even if it could, there's no way I would do that to Darlene."

"Then here's what you do. Call Eric and tell him about this place. He can send his agent to look at it and then she can find you something like it in Newport Beach."

"I bet it will cost twice as much to rent something like this in Newport."

"Well, then," Richard said, always the practical one, "you'll just have to sell twice as many wedding gowns."

"You make it sound so easy," Max said, smiling at his optimism.

"I believe in you, pumpkin."

It had been a long time since he called her pumpkin. She used to hate it when she was a kid, but now she decided she rather liked it.

"I'll have to buy a car, too. I'm going to miss walking everywhere."

"You mean when I'm not driving you or you're not borrowing my car."

"Does that bother you?"

"No, of course not. I hardly use my car. By the way," he reminded her, "I'm still starving."

Max took the hint and led him back to the car. Past the turnoff to the theater, an open stretch of land with scrub brush and scraggly looking trees lay to their right, separating the road from the ocean. They turned left away from the beach into the parking lot.

They had the choice to take a shuttle to the restaurant or walk down a long path. It was a beautiful, crisp, sunny day, so they decided to walk. The path led through trees and shrubbery to a tunnel that went under Coast Highway, and when they came out the other side, they were in another world. They walked past cottages perched on the cliffs overlooking the sea until they arrived at the Beachcomber Café. As usual on a Sunday, there was a wait, but they didn't mind relaxing on a park bench with a view of the gently crashing waves until their name was called.

After nearly an hour, they were seated outside on the patio with a view of the ocean and the children playing in the waves. Max ordered steak chilaquiles, since she believed that it was good to start the day with protein, especially when you didn't know how long your day was going to be. She would have loved a mimosa, but since she would be working at the theater later, she decided against it and ordered an orange juice. She was going to have a stiff drink as soon as they finished all the costumes. She asked them to put the orange juice in a champagne glass for her, so she didn't feel like she was completely missing out. Richard ordered poached eggs and fruit and herbal tea. Good. He was taking care of himself.

"I have something to tell you, too." Richard said, sounding very serious.

Max's stomach twisted into a knot. What was wrong? "What is it?" she asked.

"Well, it's just that, I mean, I don't really know how to say it."

"Please just say it," she pleaded, hoping it wasn't bad news. "Rip off the Band-Aid. That's what you always told me."

He laughed. "Okay. Here goes. I went on a date."

"A date?" She knew her dad would date again eventually, but she'd never be ready for it, no matter how long he waited. "With who?"

"Nancy."

"Nancy Addison from the real estate office? Really?" Richard looked at her, waiting for some sign of approval. She couldn't let him down just because she would prefer he remain celibate for the rest of his life. "She's nice," she said, pasting a smile on her face.

Richard grinned, and she could see the relief on his face. It must have been so hard to tell her. "She is. Really nice. It's nothing serious. I just wanted to go to dinner with a nice lady, so I asked her, and she said yes. I let her know that I'm not ready for anything more than casual dating. She said she was fine with that."

"Was it weird?" Max asked. "I mean, being on a date after so long?" On a date with a woman that wasn't her mom was what she wanted to say, but she held her tongue.

"Totally weird. The last first date I went on was thirty years ago. Apparently, things have changed since then, according to Nancy. She's done online dating, but I don't know what I think about that."

“So, are you going out with her again?” Max asked.

“I was thinking of asking her to see Romeo and Juliet with me.”

“That sounds nice.” Max hoped they were done talking about Richard’s love life, and luckily, he changed the subject.

He asked about Celeste and whether the detective was making any progress. Max told him the case was closed and left out the part about how she was investigating on her own.

"Peter seems to be taking Celeste’s death harder than anyone,” she said. “I guess they got really close.” She needed to talk to Peter and find out what he knew. He seemed to know Celeste better than anyone at the theater. Wouldn’t he be the most likely to know if someone wanted to do her harm?

“Peter’s a great guy. Sometimes, we guys just need someone to take us out for a beer to get us out of the house and get our minds off things. He did that for me after your mom passed away, and now I have the chance to return the favor. He never had children of his own and he liked being a father figure for Celeste.”

“You know he’s my second favorite bartender.”

Richard laughed. "You just like Burt better because he used to give you free Shirley Temples when you were a kid with about ten maraschino cherries."

"Now he gives me olives. I don't even have to order a martini. He just puts four or five on a plate for me."

"Peter doesn't need to work. He just took the job because he wanted to get out of the house a couple of nights a week. He's been retired since he moved here. It must be nice to retire so young. He's close to my age, and I'm not going to be able to retire anytime soon."

Max snickered. "Like you would ever retire. You're doing what most people do after they retire. Look at most of the people in your plein air painting group. They all started painting in their sixties or seventies."

"If I retired, I could do accounting in my free time," he grinned. "Seriously, I suppose I never will retire. Maybe I'll just start painting different subjects if I don't have to worry about them selling."

"What else would you paint?"

"I'd like to paint portraits. I've always wished I'd painted your mother when she was alive. She was such a beautiful woman."

Max could hear the love in his voice along with the pain he felt over losing the love of his life. She knew no woman would ever replace her mother in his heart.

"You've got plenty of pictures of her. Why don't you paint her portrait now?"

Richard got a faraway look in his eyes. "Maybe I will. Someday."

"Don't put things off. Life is short." She wanted her

dad to live forever. "You probably only have another forty years to live."

"Oh, so you've decided I'm going to live to be 97? Good thing I take care of myself."

Her chilaquiles were delicious and she got a box for the leftovers. She asked her dad to drop her off at the theater even though it was only eleven. There was lots of sewing still to be done.

On the drive back to the theater, she called Eric and told him about the shop she'd seen in town. Eric said Victoria had suggested the space before Eric told her Crystal Shores wasn't an option for Max's shop, so she was familiar with it.

When Max got to the theater, instead of going straight to the costume shop, she decided to check if Olivia had arrived yet. She found her in her office, her desk covered in crystals, bundles of sage, and candles.

"So, you heard about Heather's ghost sighting?" Max asked, guessing the reason for the items. "Do you think she really saw someone?"

"Like a ghost?" Olivia asked.

Max laughed. "No, of course not. But someone else could have been walking out back. It was a foggy night, so if she saw a woman through the fog, it might have looked eerie." Max had a thought. "Or maybe she feels guilty."

Olivia's eyebrows raised. "So, her conscience made her imagine she saw a ghost?"

"Okay, maybe I'm grasping at straws here. It was just a thought."

Olivia sighed heavily. "Well, I have to perform a do-it-yourself exorcism just to get her to show up to rehearsal. This is definitely not in my job description, but if something needs to be done, I'm the one to do it."

Max tried not to smile but couldn't help herself.

"Don't you laugh," Olivia warned her. "You're helping me."

"Great! Where do we get started?" She didn't know what a do-it-yourself exorcism entailed but it sounded like fun and a nice break.

"What are you so cheerful about?" Olivia asked. "I've just asked you to do more work."

"Yes," Max agreed. "But it's not sewing. I try to limit my sewing time to three or four hours max in a day, and I've been sewing ten or more hours for the last several days. Do you know what that does to your back? I seriously need a massage." When the costumes were done, she was going to take her overtime pay and visit a spa. She'd invite Keiko and Olivia along and make it a girl's day out.

"Here," Olivia said, handing Max a few pages of printed instructions. "I found this online. I would like to point out that step three is get a psychiatric evaluation. I'd like to get that girl to a shrink, but since that's not going to happen, we'll go through the motions and hopefully appease her. Also, we're not leaving her in the theater alone again."

"Good idea," Max said. "You won't have any trouble getting her to agree to that."

Olivia lit two bundles of sage, and they went around the theater letting the smoke get into all the corners, even in the offices and the costume shop. Max was glad she liked the smell, since it was likely to linger. Then Olivia placed a crystal at each entrance. Maybe it was Max's imagination, but the energy seemed lighter somehow.

"What about the candles?" Max asked. She couldn't think of anywhere they could put them where they wouldn't be a fire hazard.

"We could put them around the stage," Olivia suggested.

"So that someone's costume can catch on fire?" she said, stating the obvious.

"No, you're right." Olivia thought for a moment. "Screw the candles. Hopefully, the scent of burnt herbs will be enough to convince Heather that Celeste's ghost is gone. But what am I going to do with all these candles? I bought two dozen."

"Two dozen? That's a lot of candles."

"They were on sale," Olivia said sheepishly. "You know I can't resist a sale."

"Paint an R and a J on them and give them to the actors as opening night presents," Max suggested.

"Max, you're a genius. That's a great idea. But I'm terrible at things like that."

"Let me take them home and get my dad to do them for you," Max offered.

Olivia put all the candles in a box and handed it to Max. "Tell him he's got two seats to the play whenever he wants to come. Now that that's done, I suppose we both need to get to work."

"Shouldn't we say some words?" Max asked.

"Like, 'Hey, ghost. Get lost'?"

Max snickered. She actually had fun with their pseudo exorcism. "Hold my hands." She reached out and Olivia took both her hands in her own. "Dear Celeste. Your work here is done. It's time for you to find peace. Follow the light and join those who have gone before you."

"Okay, done," Olivia said, squeezing Max's hands before letting them drop. "Hopefully, we can get back to something close to normal." She gave Max a hug. "Thanks for helping."

Max was back in the costume shop making a list of the work they still needed to get done when Keiko arrived. "I'm sorry, I didn't bring food," Keiko said. "I had a late breakfast."

"Me, too. We'll figure out something later." She'd forgotten the leftovers in her dad's car, and hoped he put them in his refrigerator.

"The actors are starting to arrive for rehearsal," Keiko said. "They sure put in a lot of hours."

"They do when the play is due to open in a few days. Did you see Heather?"

"No, why?"

Max told her about the incident with the ghost and their attempts that morning to placate Heather by going through the motions to rid the theater of Celeste's spirit.

“I was wondering what that funny smell was,” Keiko said.

"It's burnt sage," Max explained. She looked at her list. "Okay, we've got at least a dozen more pairs of shoes to make, two more dresses to finish, not including Heather's, and the alterations on Eric's costume. That's a lot of work and not much time to do it. Shall we get to work?"

Keiko agreed and the two of them sat down and started sewing.

CHAPTER 14

Max was deep in thought as she sewed and a knock on the door made her jump. Detective Cruz entered, and she smiled when she saw him. She was looking forward to her date with Brian, but he didn't make her pulse race the way the detective did. If she thought the detective had any interest in her, would she even go out with Brian? Well, she couldn't just sit around waiting, and it was about time she started dating again. Brian was nice, and easy on the eyes, and it wasn't a big deal to go out with an old friend, was it?

She noticed the detective was holding a bag, and she hoped there was food in it.

"I brought sandwiches. I've got pastrami, turkey and ham, so I hope there's something both of you like out of those choices."

"From Joe's Deli?" Max asked. When he nodded, she said, "They make the best pastrami sandwiches!"

"Pastrami it is," Cruz said and pulled the sandwich out of the bag.

"Unless someone else wants it," Max said, trying to be unselfish. She hoped no one took her up on the offer.

"I'll take the ham, if that's okay," Keiko said, and Cruz handed her a sandwich.

"Good thing I like turkey," he said. "Of course, I bought the three kinds I like." He turned to Max. "Can we talk somewhere?"

"Sure. Let's take our lunch out to the patio in back."

Max grabbed a couple of bottles of water, and she and Cruz walked out the side door of the theater and around to the back. Behind the theater was a large patio with café tables and chairs. It had a view of the ocean and was used for opening night receptions and other events. As Max unwrapped her sandwich, she watched the sailboats out on the water gliding by.

"Are you still looking for Ivan?" she asked. "I mean, if the case is closed, and all that."

"Ivan was here illegally, so of course it's police business."

"Uh-huh." She didn't believe for a second that's why he was looking for Ivan. He'd been a loose thread in the investigation into Celeste's death that he claimed he wasn't investigating.

"I hoped to hear what you've learned," he said, changing the subject. "I know I said Celeste's death was ruled an accident, but that doesn't mean I'm not going to follow any new leads."

"What do you suspect?" she asked. "Or should I say who?"

"All the other bolts on the balcony and stairs were well tightened, and only the four bolts that held that top rail were loose. And even then, I don't see how two bolts would have come out completely, unless there were no nuts, and that makes no sense. It just seems suspicious to me. Like it was designed to make us think it was an accident. As for who I suspect, I'm not sure. But if someone is at fault, I'll find out who it was."

Max liked his determination. She admitted that she had learned little to nothing. "They always say to look at the spouse. I talked to Nathan. He works for George Biedleman, but he either didn't know anything or didn't want to tell me."

Detective Cruz told Max that George had a $1 million life insurance policy on Celeste. "That's a big policy to put on someone who earns very little money," he said. "It seems like she spent more than she made. Plus, they don't have any kids."

"Well, he's a very wealthy man, so maybe that's what rich people do," Max said.

"Maybe," he said.

"Nathan also said he went back and tightened all the nuts with a power tool," she added. "So, it seems unlikely they just fell out on their own."

The detective looked thoughtful but didn't comment. They were quiet as they ate, and then the detective asked, "So, how well do you know Kenneth?"

"I've known him since high school, when I started working for Darlene, but I haven't really spent much time with him. You know Darlene's his wife, right?" He nodded with his mouth full. "Why do you ask?"

"It's just odd that he didn't seem to care for Celeste much, but he catered to her every whim."

"Maybe that's because George was financing the play," she said.

"That's a good point."

"I've been thinking about what you said," Max said. "That it wasn't a very efficient way to kill Celeste. What if someone just wanted to hurt her? That would point to different motives, maybe different people."

"I don't think anyone was trying to kill her either. Maybe it was someone who just wanted her out of the play." Cruz gazed past her at the ocean for a moment. "Do you think Heather wanted the part badly enough to hurt Celeste?"

"I've been wondering the same thing. Could someone loosen all the nuts with their bare hands, or would you need power tools or at least a wrench?"

"Why don't we find out?" The detective stood up and threw his sandwich wrapper in the trash.

Max followed him into the theater and onto the stage. Fiona and Heather were rehearsing a scene and stopped as Max and Cruz crossed the stage behind them. Detective Cruz walked up the balcony steps to the railing with Max right behind him. The steps were narrow and steep. When she got to the top and looked down, it looked more like twenty feet to the ground, not ten. She stepped back, feeling uneasy being up here. If she felt that way, she understood why Brian wouldn't want to climb up here.

They found that the nuts on the lower railing were tightened down. They each tried loosening the nuts, but neither of them were able to with their bare hands.

"Wait here," Max told him. "I saw a workbench in the wings, and I think there's a toolbox." She found a pair of pliers and brought them back to the balcony. Cruz reached to take the pliers from her.

"Let me try," she suggested in a hushed voice. It took some effort, but she finally managed to loosen one of the nuts using the tool. "So, that means it could have been anyone."

"Even Heather," he said in a whisper.

"Yep."

They climbed down from the balcony and walked back across the stage, with Fiona and Heather watching their movements again. Before Max opened the door to the costume shop, Cruz asked, "How well do you know Brian?"

"I know you've heard all the rumors about him and Celeste, but he says there was nothing inappropriate between them. He let her flirt with him so she wouldn't get him fired. Apparently, she had that much pull with Kenneth. Brian really wants to keep this job and get his Equity card. Even Peter says there was nothing going on, and he seemed to know her better than anyone."

"So, your date with Brian is tomorrow night?" he asked.

"Yeah, he's taking me to dinner. I haven't been on a date in a long time. That is, assuming it is a date." Why was he interested in her personal life? Or were they just making friendly conversation?

“It’s a date,” he said. “I can tell by the way he looks at you. He’s interested in being more than friends.”

“Really? How come you could see that, and I couldn’t? Sometimes I think I’m just clueless when it comes to men.” She really didn't have a lot of dating experience, and most of her previous relationships hadn’t ended well. It didn’t help that she spent years in love with her childhood friend, Andy, who turned out not to return her feelings.

“That’s just part of your charm,” he said.

“I'd better get back to work," Max said, opening the door. "Thanks for lunch, Detective.” She held her hand out to shake his.

“I wish you would call me Jason,” he said, taking her hand and squeezing it gently.

“Maybe once this case is over.” Her hand tingled after he let it go. She wanted to say more to him, about how she hoped she would see him after they had learned who was responsible for Celeste’s death. She wanted to but said nothing.

“I’m going to hold you to that promise.” He turned and walked down the hall. He looked just as good walking away as he did from the front. She started to have second thoughts about her date with Brian. The man she really wanted to go out with was Detective Cruz. Why was she just realizing this now?

Stepping inside the costume shop, she got an inquisitive look from Keiko. How much had she heard?

"It looks like anyone could have loosened that nut as long as they had a wrench or a pair of pliers," Max said.

"Good to know," Keiko said. "So, did you and Jason have a good talk?"

"It seems weird to call him Jason. I think he'll always be Detective Cruz to me." In her mind, he was The Handsome Detective Cruz. But then, she read a lot of books. "I'm going to check with Olivia and see if our exorcism was successful."

"How are you going to know if the ghost is gone?" Keiko asked.

Max laughed. "Do you believe in ghosts?"

Keiko gave her a sheepish look. "Um, no. Of course not."

"As long as Heather is convinced that we did a good enough job to get rid of Celeste's ghost, then everything can go back to normal. Or whatever passes for normal around here."

CHAPTER 15

Max headed down the hallway to see Olivia. She stopped when she heard loud voices coming from Kenneth's office.

"You can't shut down the theater!" Max heard Olivia say passionately.

"I've made my decision." Kenneth's voice sounded firm. "This is going to be our last play. Sonia is raising our rent. The property management company she hired sent over a new contract today, and it's a fifty percent increase."

Max felt a little guilty listening to the private conversation, but she didn't move from her spot outside Olivia's door.

"It's a shame," Kenneth continued. "I'm finally through with Celeste and actually able to enjoy my job for the first time in years."

"Kenneth!" Olivia sounded shocked.

"I'm not glad she's dead. I'm not saying that. But her constant demands wore me out. The things I've done to keep this theater open, well, it's best if you don't know everything. But Heather…" Max could almost hear him sigh through the closed door. "Heather is such a pleasure to work with."

Max thought about the drama queen called Heather. Kenneth obviously saw another side to her.

"Just think it over before you do anything," Olivia pleaded. "I'll make some calls to our past supporters and see if I can raise some more money to keep the doors open. And if you won't talk to Sonia, then I will."

Max decided she could say hi to Olivia another time and walked quietly toward the costume shop. When she entered, Keiko gave her a funny look.

"What happened to you?" Keiko asked.

"I just overheard something I shouldn't have," Max admitted.

"I will not leave you alone until you tell me, so you might as well get it over with."

Max told Keiko that Kenneth was thinking of closing the theater.

"If he killed Celeste—"

"Keiko! I've known Kenneth for years. He couldn't possibly have done it."

"Let me finish, please. If he did kill her, then he wasn't thinking ahead, was he? So, what I am saying is if he did, it does not sound premeditated. And loosening bolts sounds like premeditation."

"Good point. Sorry. I know I should keep an open mind, but I hate to think that someone I know could do something like this."

“To solve the case, you will have to consider that possibility.”

“Detective Cruz and I were saying that whoever loosened the bolts might have actually been trying to hurt Celeste, not kill her. But I don't see why Kenneth would harm or kill Celeste. Now that she’s gone, it sounds like he’s going to have to close down the theater, so what was the point?”

Max didn’t have an answer to this or any of her other questions, so she decided to finish sewing the shoes, since it was quick work now that she had the process down. She realized they were getting low on fabric, so she gave Keiko her credit card and sent her to buy more. She reminded her to bring back the receipt so she could get Kenneth to reimburse her.

"Leave the door open when you leave," Max said. She had become uncomfortable being in the costume shop alone and having the door open made her feel better. At least it was harder for anyone to sneak up on her since she could hear the footsteps coming down the hall.

Max took the paper pattern that she had cut for Tybalt’s shoes. There were three pieces, one for the sole, one piece that covered the front of the foot, and a strip that wrapped around the back. It was quite basic, really, but looked very authentic made out of imitation leather. If the sole were made out of real leather, they could be worn to the Renaissance Faire. If Max ever wanted to start a side business, selling shoes at the Faire might be profitable.

After finishing Tybalt’s shoes, Max sat up and

stretched. She heard footsteps approaching and froze. She relaxed when Olivia came through the door. Her eyes looked red and swollen.

"Olivia, what's wrong?" Max stood up and gave her friend a hug. She had a feeling she knew what was bothering Olivia, but she pretended not to know.

"I'm not supposed to say anything, but you won't tell anyone, will you?" When Max agreed, she said, "The theater might be closing down. I'll be out of a job." Olivia started sobbing.

"Olivia, I'm so sorry. But it hasn't happened yet, right? Maybe someone will make a big donation to make up for the money George Biedleman was going to donate."

Olivia looked at her suspiciously. Oops. "What do you mean? Do you know something I don't?"

"No, I just assumed he must have pulled his funding and that's why the theater might have to close."

Olivia sat down on the sofa, looking like she'd just lost her best friend. "If he does pull out, that just makes things worse. I have to go see Sonia and try to keep her from raising our rent. I don't think she'll even listen to me. Kenneth might be able to get her to change her mind, but he refuses to go."

Max decided to change the subject. "So, what about Heather?" Max asked. "Did our exorcism convince her?"

"After tripping over a crystal and smelling the burnt sage she seemed quite cheerful. I think she'll be taking someone with her when she steps outside to smoke from now on. But I think we've taken care of that problem." Olivia saw the pile of fabric shoes on the table and said, "It looks like you're making progress on the shoes."

"Yes, I'm a shoe making machine. I think we'll be done in time after all."

"I'll let you get back to it but remember to take breaks." Olivia picked up one of the shoes, turning it over in her hands. "You've really done a great job with these."

"Thanks! And you remember not to worry about things that haven't happened yet."

"I'll try." Olivia gave her a weak smile. "It's not as easy as it sounds."

"Don't I know it!"

Max listened to Olivia's footsteps as they faded, and couldn't help but worry about her, in spite of what she'd just told her friend. There weren't many theaters in the area, and she knew Olivia wouldn't be happy unless she was involved in the theater world. If the Crystal Shores Playhouse closed, she might move to another town, and Max would miss having her friend nearby.

Keiko arrived back from the fabric store and told them that Kenneth had ordered pizza. Everyone was in the back eating. Max followed her out the stage door and around the back to the patio where at least a dozen actors happily ate pizza and chatted, enjoying their break.

Max and Keiko grabbed plates and two slices of pepperoni pizza each, then sat down with Olivia.

After they exchanged pleasantries, Keiko asked if

there was any news on Ivan, but no one had heard from him. In the meantime, Kenneth was filling in as director.

Heather came over to their table. "Can one of you open my water bottle?" she asked.

Max reached for the bottle, which opened easily.

"I have carpel tunnel," Heather said. "I'm on disability from my job doing data entry. What a horrible job that was. I've always had weak hands, but all that typing really did a number on them."

"You're allowed to take an acting job while you're on disability?" Max asked.

"I called the office, and since I'm getting paid for the role now, my disability is temporarily suspended."

Max had managed to loosen one of the nuts using a pair of pliers, but it hadn't been easy. It seemed unlikely that someone who couldn't open a water bottle would have been able to do it.

After dinner, Max and Keiko went back to work. Keiko continued working on the shoes and Max decided to finish Heather's blue dress, which was nearly done. After two hours of sewing, they were both in serious need of a break.

"Here, grab Fiona's costume," Max told Keiko, "and I'll take the blue dress. We can hand sew the hems while we watch the rehearsal." Costumes were sewn on the machine as a rule, and hand sewing hems wasn't as quick as doing them on the machine, but Max found it very relaxing. Plus, she'd never sat in on a rehearsal before.

They found seats in the third row where the

lighting was decent, threaded their needles, and sewed as they listened. Max looked up from her task to see Kenneth on stage with Heather and Brian, rehearsing the fateful balcony scene.

Heather was inspecting the inside of the balcony, and Kenneth asked her what she was doing.

"I don't want the same thing happening to me that happened to Celeste," she said. "I don't have an understudy, so that would be the end of the production."

"We had the balcony rebuilt and reinforced and brought in an inspector to make sure it's safe," Kenneth informed her.

"I just want to make sure," Heather said.

"All right," Kenneth said impatiently. "Let me know when you're done."

Heather seemed satisfied, so they began the scene, but she stayed back from the railing. Max was impressed with Brian's acting skills. He delivered Shakespeare's words effortlessly and moved around the stage as if he had always belonged there. He looked up at Juliet just like a lovesick teenager, and Max could completely understand why Juliet immediately fell in love with Romeo. She wasn't getting much of the hem done since she was preoccupied with watching Brian and letting her mind wander. What should she wear for her date tomorrow?

Kenneth stopped the rehearsal and walked over to the base of the balcony and inspected it. "How are you supposed to climb up?" he asked Brian.

"I don't climb up," Brian said.

“Ivan is having you do the entire scene from the base of the balcony? Did he happen to say why?”

“It’s my fault, actually,” Brian admitted. “I’m afraid of heights. I told him I’d have to quit the production if I had to climb the balcony.”

Kenneth shook his head in frustration. “You’re lucky, then. I would have found another actor. But it’s too late now.”

Brian was afraid of heights. Max smiled. It was as good as an alibi. She wondered if Detective Cruz knew. Of course, she hadn’t thought for a minute that Brian had tried to injure Celeste. Then she scowled. If it wasn’t Heather or Brian who rigged the balcony, she was running out of suspects. Still, she only needed one, and hopefully that person was the guilty party.

Max was startled by a booming voice that called out from the back of the theater, “Kenneth, we need to talk.” A portly man who appeared to be in his fifties walked up the center aisle. Max didn’t recognize him, noting his pasty complexion and bushy mustache.

“George,” Kenneth said, climbing down the stage steps and meeting George in front of the stage. “How are you doing? I left you a message with my condolences. We all feel Celeste’s loss, but you more than anyone, of course.”

Celeste’s husband. What was he doing here?

“One of your actors stole her ring,” he said angrily. “I want it back now or I’m calling the police.”

CHAPTER 16

"What are you talking about?" Kenneth asked.

"Her wedding ring," George said. "A four-carat flawless diamond. It cost me a bundle. She was wearing it when she left the house, and the hospital says she wasn't wearing it when she arrived there."

"Surely you don't think—" Kenneth began.

"Yes, I do." He turned toward the stage and addressed the actors. "One of you is a thief!"

The actors stared at George and said nothing.

"I'm calling the cops then." He pulled out his phone, but before he dialed, he said, "And this is as good a time as any to tell you I'm pulling out of the play."

"But…" Kenneth began. "Can we talk about this? Your support means everything to the theater."

"The decision's been made," George said firmly. "I only supported this money pit because of Celeste. Now that she's gone, I'm done."

Brian walked down the stage steps and headed toward the two men. "George, don't you think Celeste would have wanted you to continue supporting the play?"

"You!" George shouted. When Brian was close enough, the big man grabbed him by his shirt collar. "You made a fool of me. Well, you're not going to do it anymore." He shoved Brian, who fell back against the stage, then George turned and stomped out of the theater. Everyone stood still and silent watching him leave.

"Okay, back to work, everyone," Kenneth said, clapping his hands. Quietly, he asked Brian, "Are you okay?"

"Yeah, I'm fine." Brian frowned and glanced over where Max was sitting. He walked back up the stairs to the stage and took his place near the balcony.

"Romeo, Romeo," Heather began.

Rehearsal was certainly much more interesting than Max had thought it would be. She leaned over to Keiko and whispered, "Do you have your laptop with you?"

"Always," Keiko answered.

"Why don't you see what you can find out about George?"

Keiko nodded and slipped out of the auditorium. Peter came over and sat next to her, whispering, "How are you enjoying the rehearsal?"

"Brian is a really good actor, isn't he?"

"Yes, he's quite good," Peter said. "And what about Heather?"

Max didn't know quite what to say. "Well..."

"I didn't mean to put you on the spot. Everyone thinks she's a terrible actor. But she's all we've got. For everything you might say about Celeste, and I know she wasn't your favorite, she was quite talented. We were very lucky to have someone of her caliber at our little theater."

Max wondered how to bring up the fact that she knew Celeste was his daughter. He had his reasons for keeping it a secret. Maybe he would be uncomfortable if she brought it up. But she had another subject to ask him about. "You helped build the sets, didn't you?"

"Nathan and I built most of the balcony set. The other sets were just moveable flats, which only took a day to construct." He must have seen the blank look on Max's face because he explained, "moveable flats are walls built to stand at the back of the stage. They're painted with the scenery, and then they can be moved easily when the scene changes."

"I see," Max said. The theater world was interesting, with its own rules and language. "Could any of the nuts have been left loose or missing on the balcony railing? Maybe it was overlooked?"

"No way," Peter said confidently. "Nathan tightened down all the nuts with his power drill. I remember him doing it."

"Sounds to me like it wasn't an accident then." That meant her suspicions had been right all along. "Do you know anyone who might have wanted to harm Celeste?"

"I've been asking myself the same question. She didn't get along with everyone, or much of anyone, really. I mean, she was a bit of a diva." He smiled, remembering, and then blinked as if to keep the tears from coming. "But I don't remember any arguments." He stood up. "I'll give it some more thought," he said and went backstage.

Heather and Brian ran through the balcony scene several times, and Heather never got too close to the railing as she said her lines. Kenneth tried to convince her to be less dramatic in her delivery, but she said her lines the same each time and he finally gave up.

They rehearsed several more scenes, and when Max yawned, she looked at her phone to see the time. It was after eleven. How long would they be rehearsing? Her eyes were too tired to sew any more tonight, so she gathered the dress and her things and stood up, ready to return to the costume shop.

Max heard the front door open, and Detective Cruz walked up the aisle with Officer Daniels. He went up to Kenneth and handed him a piece of paper, which Max guessed was a search warrant. She watched as Kenneth read it, unable to decipher his reaction. When someone as prominent in the community as George Biedleman made an accusation, apparently the police took it seriously.

"Everyone, please stay here while we search the premises," Detective Cruz announced.

The actors all seemed uncomfortable, but if anyone was guilty of stealing Celeste's ring, it wasn't obvious to Max. She thought back to the night Celeste fell. Peter was the first person at her side, taking her pulse, and then Fiona took over and performed CPR until the two paramedics arrived. Those four people were the only ones who could have stolen the ring, unless the theft happened at the hospital. Max didn't believe any of them were capable of it. But Celeste had been wearing the ring that night, that much Max knew for sure. She'd seen it for herself.

Max hoped it wouldn't take them long to search the theater since she could hardly keep her eyes open. She wanted nothing more than to go home and go to sleep. When Detective Cruz returned to the auditorium he came over to where she was sitting and quietly asked to talk to her. She led the way to the costume shop.

"We didn't find the ring," he said, "but I didn't expect to. What do you remember from that night? Who was close enough to Celeste to take the ring?"

Max thought back to the moments when she first ran out to the theater and saw Celeste's lifeless body lying on the stage. "The only people I remember near her were Peter, Fiona, and the paramedics, but it can't be any of them, can it? Maybe it went missing at the hospital." She was too tired to try to make sense of everything.

"How well do you know Peter and Fiona?" he asked.

"I've known them both for years. I know Fiona better than Peter, since her shop is next door to ours. She pops in all the time to say hi. Fiona's lived in town for over twenty years and Peter for at least five, I think. He's friends with my dad."

"I'll have to question both of them. You can go home if you want. I know it's late."

"I want to stay and see if you find out anything."

The detective scowled at her. “I tried asking nicely, but I really must insist you go home. I’m sending everyone home except Peter and Fiona.” He noticed the plate of snickerdoodles. "Ooh, cookies," he said, his demeanor completely changing. "May I?"

"Yes, please, take them all."

"You don't like cookies?" he asked. "Who doesn't like cookies?"

"I'm just cutting back on sweets," she fibbed. Maybe the cookies weren’t as bad as she thought they were. Or did Detective Cruz have really bad taste in cookies? He could be one of those people who ate anything. Max had heard about people like that, but it mystified her, being such a picky eater herself.

“One more thing,” Max said as she gathered up her things. “Peter saw Nathan tighten the bolts on the railing, so they couldn’t possibly have come out on their own.”

“Why didn’t Peter tell me that when I questioned him?”

“Maybe he didn’t think it was important at the time.”

“Maybe,” he said, but didn’t sound convinced. “Well, goodnight,” he said. He waited a moment as if he had something else to say and then left.

When Max went to turn off her sewing machine, she noticed a note propped up on it.

Lots of dirt so far. Will update you in the A.M.

Well, that was intriguing. Was Keiko talking about George? Surely, she hadn’t heard about the missing ring yet.

She looked at the clock on the wall and realized it was after one. No wonder Keiko had gone home. It was time for her to do the same, but she didn't have a ride home. It was unlike Keiko to leave her stranded like that.

A knock on the door interrupted her thoughts. Brian entered.

"Keiko texted Fiona that she forgot you would need a ride home, so I volunteered. I hope you don't mind."

"Not at all," Max said, although she knew Keiko would have never forgotten. It was probably Keiko's and Fiona's idea to throw her and Brian together.

Once they were in the parking lot, Brian led her to his two-year-old Honda. Good, he was practical. Not flashy like her last boyfriend. Brian opened the door for her.

"That's crazy about the ring, right?" Brian said. "Why did that police detective want to talk to you?"

"He wanted to know who was close enough to Celeste that night to take the ring."

"I think he likes you," Brian said. "Should I be jealous?"

"Of Detective Cruz? Don't be ridiculous." The detective had never given any indication that he was interested in her. Or had he? He often seemed annoyed with her. She changed the subject. "I never knew you were afraid of heights."

"I've always kept it quiet, but Celeste knew back when we were in high school. She lured me to the roof of the boys' gym one time, pretending she was interested in me, then challenged me to look over the side.

When I couldn't do it, she called me a scaredy-cat." He chuckled. "It sounds silly now, but she teased me mercilessly all through senior year. She even got some of the other kids to call me that."

"She was mean to me, too, in middle school. I know the feeling of having other kids calling you names when you're walking down the hall. I was lucky enough that she and her friends never talked to me by the time I got to high school."

"You're right. You were lucky." They drove in silence for a few minutes, and then Brian said, "Is the detective still looking into Celeste's death?"

"Her death has been ruled an accident." Max decided not to tell him she was investigating on her own. He might not understand why she felt the need to get to the bottom of it.

"But you don't think it was an accident," he said.

"It doesn't really matter what I think. The case is closed."

They pulled up in front of Max's home. "So, I'll see you tomorrow." He reached out and squeezed her hand. "Dress comfortably. I can't afford a fancy restaurant. I hope you don't mind."

"Of course not," Max said, honestly. She liked fancy restaurants as much as any woman who loved food, but she wasn't looking for a rich boyfriend. Just a nice one. Someone she could talk to and share all her secrets with. Here she was thinking about Brian as a possible boyfriend, and she wasn't even sure if it was a date. What was it that her dad used to tell her? Slow down, turbo.

The lights were out in her dad's house, so she walked around the side and up the stairs to her apartment. She was exhausted. When she took off her sweater, she felt something heavy in the pocket. She reached in and pulled out a very large diamond ring.

CHAPTER 17

Max's phone buzzed at seven, waking her up. She found a text from Keiko.

Meet me at Rose Street Cafe at 8:30?

What was up with people waking her up so early? She answered the text and then sat up, remembering the ring. First, she needed to call Detective Cruz. She really didn't want to answer questions about how it got in her pocket until she figured it out for herself, or at least until she had some coffee and was more awake.

She did some of her best thinking in the shower. Who could have put the ring in her pocket? Brian had driven her home. Why would he have had the ring in the first place, and then why slip it into her pocket? Earlier in the evening, she had been sitting in the audience with Keiko. Then Keiko had left, and Peter sat next to her. Peter. Could he be the one who planted the ring on her? She decided to send Detective Cruz a text instead of calling, letting him know he could pick up the ring from her dad.

She stopped in to say good morning to her dad and let him know she wouldn't be joining him for coffee and oatmeal. "Would you hold onto this for me?" she asked, handing him the ring.

"Is there something I should know?" he asked, raising his eyebrows.

"Yes, I'm getting married," she joked, but when she saw his jaw drop, she quickly added, "Just kidding! It's Celeste's ring. Someone stole it the night she died and then put it in my pocket last night."

"Well, that's odd," he said. "Who do you think put it there?"

Peter was the first person who came to mind, but she didn't want to jump to conclusions. "I really don't know," she said.

"I'll put it in the safe."

"We have a safe?" This was news to her.

"*I* have a safe," he said, smiling. "It's where I keep all my ill-gotten gains."

"Okay, if you say so," she said, knowing that the closest thing her dad had to ill-gotten gains was the money he won at poker. "I told Detective Cruz, he could pick it up from you. I hope that's okay."

"Sure. It will give us a chance to talk about how he keeps getting my daughter involved in his murder investigations."

"Dad, please don't." Max hoped he wasn't being serious.

"I'm not promising anything."

Rose Street Cafe was only a few blocks away, and it was a cool summer morning, perfect for a walk. Max found Keiko on the patio with two cappuccinos. Keiko had learned all of Max's favorite things to eat and drink over the past several months and was very good at indulging her.

Max told her about the stolen ring that had ended up in her pocket. She decided to confide her suspicions to Keiko.

"Here's the thing. Only Peter and Fiona were next to Celeste after she fell. And then, last night, Peter came and sat next to me. I think he slipped the ring into my pocket in case he was searched."

"No!" Keiko said, her eyes getting bigger. "Do you really think so?"

"It's the only thing that makes sense. I want a chance to talk to Peter before I tell Detective Cruz anything. I want to hear his side of the story." She had trouble believing Peter was capable of stealing a ring off an unconscious woman, but she couldn't think of another explanation. "Anyway, what did you want to tell me?"

Keiko opened her laptop on the table while Max took a sip of her cappuccino and sighed. There was nothing like the first taste of coffee in the morning.

"So, here's what I learned about George Beidleman," Keiko began. "Beidleman Construction was started by his father decades ago, and he worked for the company while he was going through college. I'm not sure what he did for them, but I think he was just a laborer. Then he dropped out of college." Keiko took a sip of her cappuccino and looked at the laptop screen. "He had an older brother named Arnold who fell off the roof at a construction site and died. Right after that, their father retired, and George took over the business. This was all twenty years ago."

"His brother died from a fall?" Max could tell Keiko knew what she was thinking. "That's quite a coincidence."

"You mean that his brother and wife both died from a fall? I was thinking the same thing."

This was something Detective Cruz needed to know, if he didn't already. She pulled her phone out of her purse to call him and noticed there were two missed calls from him, including a voice message. She hadn't heard it ringing in the noisy restaurant.

"I'd better listen to this," she told Keiko. In the detective's message he asked for an explanation about the ring, but she didn't have one yet. She decided to wait to tell him about George.

"Great work, Keiko," Max said. "How about I buy you breakfast? Their poached eggs on toast is awesome."

"I would like that."

After breakfast, Keiko dropped off Max at the theater and headed for the bridal shop, since Darlene asked her to come in early. Keiko was a part-time employee, but since school was out for the summer, she didn't mind working more hours. She was saving up to take a trip to Japan for the first time. She hadn't seen her Japanese father in several years. Her mother, who was not Japanese, had raised her as a single mother, and she'd seen little of her father growing up. Technology made it easier to keep in touch these days, but it was not the same as seeing someone in person.

Max knew she was also excited about visiting Japan, which was a dream of hers. Keiko had embraced her Japanese heritage when she grew up, even changing her name from Cathy.

Max had plenty of work to do, but she had a nagging thought that wouldn't go away. Why would Peter steal Celeste's ring? She got on the ancient desktop computer that sat in a corner of the costume shop and googled his name, but she couldn't find much of an online presence for him. The little she'd found didn't go back more than five years ago, which was around the time he'd come to Crystal Shores.

"I bet Keiko can find more information about you, Peter," she said out loud. She accepted that Keiko was much better at all the computer stuff than she was. Keiko had been a computer science major before she decided to go to design school, and still did consulting and website design.

Max got back to work sewing until Keiko arrived at noon with lentil soup from Chez Mer. Max grabbed her sweater and they took their lunch out to the back patio. The sun was shining in a sky dotted with fluffy, white clouds, but the sea breeze kept the temperature under seventy degrees.

"We need to get you a new sweater," Keiko said with a distasteful look on her face. "I hate that thing."

"What's wrong with it?" Max was very attached to her sweater, which was soft and almost as cuddly as a security blanket. "It's practical."

"It's shapeless and boring."

"But black goes with everything." Max's sweater

was like an old pair of comfortable slippers that you kept until they fell apart. Her sweater was still in decent shape and just the right weight for Southern California.

“When we're done with these costumes, we're going shopping again and getting something to replace it,” Keiko said firmly.

Since shopping with Keiko was an adventure that anyone would be lucky to experience, Max didn't argue, even if it meant giving up her old sweater.

"Can we go to L.A. again?" Max asked.

"Of course, we're going to L.A. Where else?"

Max asked Keiko if she thought Peter could have stolen the ring.

“Isn’t he a friend of your dad’s?” Keiko asked. “How long have you known him?”

“I’ve known him for years, but I don’t really know much about him. Like what he did before he came to Crystal Shores. He said he retired from some kind of boring job, but I don’t remember what. Accounting, maybe. Or he was an actuary. I’m not sure what he said. I suppose if he had a criminal record, the police would have discovered that after they took everyone’s fingerprints.”

“Would that detective tell you if he did?”

Max frowned. “I hope so,” she said, but she wasn’t sure.

After they finished their lunch and went back inside, Max called Detective Cruz, who scolded her for not returning his calls and texts. She’d been thinking since breakfast about what to tell him. She’d hoped she would have figured it out by now, but she couldn't put off talking to him any longer.

He questioned her about the ring, but she told him honestly that she didn't know how it got in her pocket. She wasn't ready to share her suspicions about Peter.

Max asked if anyone at the theater had a record, not naming Peter, but he said he couldn't tell her that information. Then he said there wasn't anything to tell anyway, so she took that to mean that no one, including Peter, had a record.

Max went back to sewing and Keiko pulled out her laptop. Eventually, Keiko gave up on her research and helped Max with the costumes.

CHAPTER 18

Max and Keiko heard the actors start to arrive as Max finished another pair of shoes. Peter hadn't been around when she was tracing everyone else's feet, so she went out to the stage to look for him. Not only did she want to finish his shoes, but also, she wanted to hear what he had to say about the ring.

She didn't see Peter, so she told Kenneth to send him to her when he arrived. Fiona followed her back to the costume shop carrying Josie.

"Has Josie caught a single mouse?" Max had to speak up to be heard over the sewing machine as Keiko sewed.

"I don't think so," Fiona said, "but we haven't seen any since I've been bringing her. I think they're hiding from her."

"Well, I suppose that's almost as good. And not as grisly. I was hoping she wasn't going to bring us any dead mice." Max looked at the cat who had a disinterested look on her face. "Does she miss Simon and Teresa?"

"I'm sure she misses Teresa. That cat loves my sister. Oh," she said, putting Josie down and pulling her phone out of her pocket. "I got an email from Teresa. Do you girls want to hear what she said?"

Keiko stopped sewing and looked up. "Sure," she said.

"How are the two lovebirds doing?" Max asked.

"It sounds like they're having a wonderful time. Here's the email: Blah, blah, weather, blah, blah, showing him around Edmonton, oh, here's the good part. 'Simon refused to stay at my place, since he didn't want my neighbors talking, so he booked a room at the Fairmont. The Fairmont! That place is a fortune. He's taken me out to dinner every night this week, but I insisted on cooking for him tonight. Tomorrow, we're driving to Banff, and Simon's booked two rooms at the Chateau.' Have you ever been to Alberta, Max?"

Max admitted she'd never been to Canada.

"Lake Louise and Banff are absolutely beautiful. They're both in the Canadian Rockies. You really must go and visit Teresa while she's still spending summers in Edmonton. I suspect that Simon will propose soon, and she'll be moving to California permanently."

"That would be wonderful. They make such a cute couple."

"I think it's great that they found love later in life." Keiko added.

"Any men in your life, Fiona?" Max asked.

"Just my son in law and my grandson. They're all I

need. I had a wonderful marriage, but I don't mind being on my own. Men can be a pain. When you get married, you'd better make sure you're in love or you'll be miserable."

"I feel like I should needlepoint that on a pillow."

Fiona laughed. "Well, it's true. Don't you go falling for just any pretty face. You hold out for the one. Promise me."

"I promise," Max said.

"Speaking of people's love lives, have you noticed how Olivia looks at Zach?" Max looked at her blankly and Fiona reminded her, "He's playing Tybalt."

"No, I haven't noticed. Do you think there's something going on there?" Max felt a little guilty talking about Olivia behind her back, but if there was a new man in her life, she really wanted to know. He was the one who had been lurking about. Maybe this explained why.

"He's an environmental lawyer," Fiona said, "and I think he only auditioned for the play to be around Olivia. She keeps telling people she's too busy to date, but I think the truth is she doesn't want to get close to anyone."

"She doesn't open up easily," Max said. "She's told me very little about her childhood, and I think I'm her best friend. I suppose she'll tell me about this new guy when she's ready. If there's something to tell."

"Oh, there's definitely something to tell," Fiona said.

Max was uncomfortable talking about Olivia's love life, but she was a little hurt that Olivia hadn't confided in her. She decided to change the subject. "Are you rehearsing every day this week?"

"Yes, there's a rehearsal for everyone tonight but Brian and Heather. The understudies are doing a run through tonight, plus it gives the lead actors a chance to rest their voices. Besides, Brian needs the night off for his date."

"But Heather doesn't have an understudy."

"Olivia will be filling in for her tonight. She can read from the script, although as many times as she'd heard them rehearse, she probably knows the part by heart. So, are you excited for your date? Brian's very handsome."

"I'm a little excited," Max fibbed. She was very excited, but still distracted thinking about the stolen ring.

She realized she needed to get home to change her clothes, so her confrontation with Peter would have to wait. She was glad Brian had told her to dress casually. She thought it was very considerate of him to let her know how to dress. She hated getting ready to go out not knowing what to wear. The worst was going to a party and realizing that everyone was wearing jeans when you had put on a cute dress. Or vice versa. How did everyone else know how they were supposed to dress, and she didn't?

Fiona interrupted her reverie. "Isn't it about time you got out of here? What time is he picking you up?"

"At seven, and you're right. I do need to get going." She walked over to the sofa where Josie had curled up and scratched her behind one ear. "I guess you won't get to spend this evening in my lap."

"No, Josie," Fiona said. "Her lap belongs to someone else for tonight."

"Fiona!" Max exclaimed, but Fiona only laughed and headed back out to the stage.

Max had her purse over her shoulder, ready to leave when Peter finally showed up. He seemed agitated.

"Is everything all right?" Max asked him, putting her purse down.

"I just need to get through the night without punching Kenneth in the face." As if to illustrate, he punched one fist into his other hand repeatedly.

"Has he done something?" Max asked, not understanding where all this anger was coming from.

"He's glad she's dead," Peter said, and when Max started to protest, he said, "I can just tell it. He's so happy working with Heather. And there are just little things he says."

"Like what?"

"Oh, I don't know. Just talking about how easy Heather is to work with. He dotes on her. I wouldn't be surprised if he was the one who killed Celeste."

"Wait a minute, Peter," Max said, trying to be the voice of reason. "What possible motive would he have? Now that she's dead, George has pulled his support and the theater might close down."

"Maybe he didn't think that far ahead. Or he didn't want Celeste to tell his wife about his gambling debts."

"Whoa, hold on there." She didn't see that coming. "What?"

Peter sighed deeply. "I shouldn't have said anything. I'm just so angry." He walked over to the sofa and collapsed into it. Max waited for him to continue. "He had a gambling problem years ago. He and Darlene almost split up over it. It could end his marriage if Darlene found out that he was gambling again."

"How do you even know this?" Max didn't think Kenneth would have confided such personal information with Peter. As far as Max knew, they weren't particularly close.

"Celeste told me. He had asked her for a loan. She said she wanted to know why he needed the money before she'd give it to him. She said he seemed pretty desperate."

"How much money does he owe?" Max regretted the question as soon as she'd said it. This was her boss's husband. She didn't want to know about his personal vices.

"More than he can pay. You can't say anything," Peter said. "Celeste made me promise not to tell anyone, but I thought you should know. Darlene's the one with the money, from what I've heard."

"I've heard that, too, from Darlene, in fact. She had a successful career as an investment banker before she retired and opened Wedding Belles. That's around the same time she married Kenneth."

"So, you'll look into it?" Peter asked.

"I'm looking into everyone," Max assured him, and Peter turned to go. "Wait. I have a question to ask you."

"What is it?" Peter turned back around to face her.

"I found Celeste's ring in my pocket last night." She

felt awkward asking the question, but she knew she had to. "Did you put it there?"

"What?" Peter said in a shocked voice. "Do you think I stole it?"

"Well…" Max paused. "Did you?"

"I can't believe you would think such a thing." He sounded indignant.

"I'm sorry. I had to ask."

Peter turned and walked out of the room without another word. There must be another explanation. Someone else must have stolen the ring. But how did it end up in her sweater pocket? Peter had been doing community theater ever since he came to Crystal Shores. How good of an actor was he?

CHAPTER 19

There was a knock on Max's front door promptly at seven. She loved it when people were on time. She opened the door, letting Brian in.

"How about showing me around?" He asked.

"It's a really short tour," she said. She loved her sunny apartment, but it was tiny. "Here's the living room and dining room, and over there is my little kitchen." She opened her bedroom door. "And there's my bedroom and bath. That's about it." She felt awkward showing him her bedroom, but at least she'd made the bed this morning. "Ready to go?"

"I'm glad to see you're wearing comfortable shoes."

"Are you going to tell me where we're going?"

"You'll find out in due time," he said, winking.

When he turned off Coast Highway onto Jamboree, she realized they were going to Balboa, either the island or the peninsula. Brian found a place to park on the island, and they walked along the sidewalks past frozen yogurt shops and souvenir stores. They got to the ferry and walked on. Max hadn't taken the ferry to the peninsula in years, and it was the perfect evening for it, still warm with a cool ocean breeze.

Several cars drove onto the ferry, and they sat on a bench along the side. It took just a few minutes to get to the other side, and when they stepped off the ferry, they were in the middle of the Balboa Fun Zone.

"Hungry?" Brian asked.

"You bet!" Max said, hoping for the best.

"Pizza or hot dogs?"

"Hot dogs. Definitely. Darlene orders pizza every time she makes me work through lunch. I'm kind of sick of it." She looked at Brian who seemed to be pouting. "Unless you want pizza," she quickly added.

Brian laughed. "I hate pizza. I was just teasing a little. I hope you don't mind." Max shook her head. "Now that I know how you really feel about pizza, how do you feel about corn dogs?"

"Love them!"

They strolled along the walkway, past souvenir shops and food vendors until they came to a storefront with a sign proclaiming, "Fortunes Told. Palms Read. Tarot Cards." Max stopped in her tracks when she saw what was written on the door. "Madam Giana." She stared at the name. This was the fortuneteller Celeste had seen before she died.

"Don't tell me you believe in this stuff," Brian said in a teasing voice. When she didn't respond he said, "I mean, it's okay if you do."

"I have to go in," Max said and pushed on the door to enter before he could react. Brian followed her inside. The small room held two brocade armchairs between which was a round table with an ornate bell. A sign said, "Ring for assistance." Max picked up the bell and shook it gently.

A woman emerged from the curtains in the back of the space. Her dark hair fell wildly past her shoulders and her long, colorful skirt swished as she walked.

"You have come to ask me a question," she said in a vague European accent.

"Well, yes, actually," Max said, taken aback. "Are you Madam Giana?"

"Yes. Come with me." She turned, clearly expecting Max to follow her. Over her shoulder, she called, "He cannot join us." Max looked back at Brian who just shrugged. She parted the curtains to an even smaller space. "His energy will confuse the reading." She motioned for Max to sit down across from her at a little table covered in crystals and candles.

Max took in the dark red, flocked wallpaper and ornately framed pictures of angels and other apparently supernatural beings. "You did a reading for a woman named Celeste," she began.

"Forty dollars for a three-card reading," the woman said, holding out her hand. "Past, present, and future."

"But I just have a question for you," Max protested.

"Forty dollars," the woman said firmly. "Cash."

Max dug in her purse and found her wallet, pulling out two twenties.

After handing over the money, Madam Giana took her deck of Tarot cards and spread them in a semicircle on the table. "Mix them up, and then when you are ready, put them in a stack. Think of your question as you do it."

Max obeyed and when she was done presented the woman with the deck.

Madam Giana took the top three cards and placed them in front of her.

"First, I turn over the center card, which represents the present." After turning it over, she gave a slight gasp, then quickly recovered. The card was death.

"Do not be alarmed," she said, although she clearly was. "The meaning of this card is nearly always symbolic. Unless someone near you has died recently?"

"Yes, that's why I came. You did a reading for Celeste and she's dead now. You told her she would die."

Madam Giana swallowed but said nothing, just turned over the card to her right.

Max could feel her frustration build. She just spent forty dollars to find out what this "fortune teller" had meant by what she'd told Celeste. It was probably nothing more than coincidence, and now Max felt a little stupid being here, expecting answers from this woman who was probably no more than entertainment for tourists.

"Eight of cups," Madam Giana said. "This means you will leave something, perhaps a job or a relationship. I feel that there is an opportunity for you."

Max decided to play along. Maybe she would get further that way. "I might be starting my own business."

"Yes, that is what I am seeing. You have regrets

about leaving your current job, but it is the right move for you."

This was all very interesting, but it wasn't the answer she was looking for right now. She scolded herself. There were no such things as psychics. Why was she really here? Did a part of her believe this woman could really tell the future?

Finally, the last card was turned over. The past.

"This card represents something in the past that is helping or holding you back from your destination. Seven of wands. Someone is not what they seem. I fear you are close to someone who is lying to you, and you are unable to see the truth."

"By close, do you mean close in proximity or close in a relationship sense?"

"It could be either. That is all the cards tell me."

Max sighed. This was pointless. "Well, thank you," Max said, standing up. "By the way, what did you mean when you told Celeste a nut would kill her?"

"I don't remember saying that, but I'm not surprised she's dead." Madam Giana stood up also and tossed her long, unruly hair over her shoulder casually, but there was an edge in her voice. "I sensed someone was very jealous. You won't tell the police about me, will you, hon? We have a bit of a shaky relationship," she said, shrugging. "It's all due to a misunderstanding, of course."

"Of course," Max said.

Before Max could turn to leave, Madam Giana closed her eyes. When she opened them, she had a faraway look in her eyes. Without a hint of an accent, she said, *"Fate has a sense of humor and just when you think you have the life you have dreamed of, you will find that what you believe is just a mirage. Never ignore your inner voice. It holds the truth."*

She blinked twice and looked at Max as if wondering why she was still there. Max went back into the front room where Brian waited for her.

"You okay?" Brian asked.

Max laughed awkwardly. "Of course. Thank you for indulging me."

"No problem. What did the fortune teller tell you?"

"Oh, just the usual," Max said, not wanting to share the details with him until she had a chance to think. "I'm going to live a long and happy life." She hoped he wouldn't push for more.

"Well, that's good to hear. Now for the best corn dog you've ever had. How about a beer to wash it down with?"

They ate their corn dogs standing at a table overlooking the bay. The sun was beginning to set behind them and lights were turning on at all the shops and amusements.

"You've got a little mustard, right there," Brian said, pointing to a corner of Max's mouth. "Wait, I've got it." He took a napkin and leaned in to wipe it off. He was very close, and Max resisted the impulse to pull away. She hadn't been face to face like this with a man in quite a while. He was near enough to kiss her, and she wondered if he would. She didn't have to wonder long. Brian gave her a quick soft kiss.

"I've wanted to do that for years," Brian said shyly. "It was worth the wait."

"I'm glad to hear that," Max said, and then mentally kicked herself. What a stupid thing to say! *I'm glad to hear that.* Why couldn't she ever think of the right thing to say when she was put on the spot?

"Is everything all right?" Brian asked.

"Better than all right," she said, and gave him what she hoped was a warm smile. "How about I treat for dessert. Ice cream or cotton candy?"

"What, no frozen banana?"

"No way! If you want a frozen banana, you have to pay for it yourself. The only dessert I approve of that includes bananas is a banana split. And then I just eat around the bananas and leave them behind in the empty dish."

They agreed on ice cream cones and ate them walking along the path and looking in the windows of the souvenir shops. Brian caught her admiring a seashell necklace and asked her to hold his cone for a moment. He went inside and came out a short time later, putting the necklace over her head.

"I want you to have something to help you remember this night," he said after she thanked him.

"Don't worry. I won't forget it." She reached out and took his hand. He wove his fingers through hers.

Brian had to work at his day job the next morning, so they got back on the ferry and rode it back to the island. On the drive home, Brian told her about his job working for a local interior design studio.

"I'm pretty much a gofer, doing whatever they need

done from delivering sofas to sweeping up," he said. "I don't mind because my boss is flexible with my hours so I can do theater. That's always been my first love, ever since I was a kid."

"Why didn't you do any shows in high school?" Max asked.

"I tried out, but they only picked the popular kids. Or maybe it was because I was fat."

"You weren't fat," Max protested. "Just a little..." She realized whatever she said was going to come out wrong.

"Pudgy? That's okay. You can say it. I could whine about being pudgy and unpopular in high school, or I could be thankful that I have the life I have now, on a date with a beautiful woman."

Max felt her cheeks redden and was relieved that they had reached her home. Brian walked her up to her front door at the top of the stairs and said he couldn't stay, saving her from having to decide whether to invite him in or not.

Brian stroked the side of her cheek and gave her another soft kiss, this one slightly longer than the first. Then he turned around and practically ran down the stairs. At the bottom, he turned around and grinned.

"See you tomorrow!"

CHAPTER 20

Max woke up Tuesday morning with a smile on her face, wanting to just lie in bed all day thinking about her date with Brian. His kisses stayed in her mind—so soft and gentle. He was really sweet. She'd almost forgotten all about Detective Cruz. Darn! Why was she thinking about him now?

Eventually, she got out of bed, daydreaming while she showered and dressed. She took a little more time with her hair and makeup. She wanted to look nice when she saw Brian later at the theater. She was headed out the door when she remembered the shell necklace and pulled it on over her head.

She went downstairs and walked through the back door of her dad's house into his kitchen. She poured herself a cup of coffee, but there was no oatmeal in the rice cooker. She was looking through the cupboards when her dad walked in.

"Raiding the pantry, I see," he said.

"Well, I'm trying," she confessed, "but I haven't been very successful so far."

"That's because you haven't looked in the breadbasket." Richard pulled out a white paper bag. "I got you a cinnamon raisin bagel. I know it's your favorite." He popped the bagel into the toaster along with one for himself.

"Thanks, Dad. I'll get out the butter."

"So, how was your date last night?" he asked.

"How did you know—" Max stopped and turned to him. "I wasn't keeping it a secret from you."

"You used to tell me everything."

"When was that?" she laughed. "When I was twelve? It's just that I wasn't even sure it was a date, and I didn't want to tell you until I knew for sure."

"I'm guessing by the grin on your face that it turned out to be a date."

"Yep. Definitely a date." She couldn't stop smiling.

"Were you afraid to tell me you were going out with a murder suspect?"

Max's smile faded. She couldn't tell by his tone of voice if he were being sarcastic or not. "He's not a suspect. Not on my list, anyway. He's really nice and I don't think he would hurt a fly." She hoped she didn't sound defensive. "Besides, he's afraid of heights, so there's no way he climbed up on that rickety balcony to remove a screw."

"I didn't mean to rain on your parade. I'm glad you had a nice time." He put the toasted bagels on plates and started buttering them. "I had a nice evening also. I had Peter over for dinner. I knew he was upset about

Celeste's death, so I thought he could use some company. Besides, I wanted some company, too. I'm still not used to eating dinner alone."

"I know, Dad. Sorry I haven't been around much lately."

"I understand. You need to have a life of your own. Peter thinks Kenneth rigged the balcony, but he wouldn't tell me why he thinks so. If he did, I don't know how anyone could prove it."

"I don't know how anyone is going to prove anything." Max felt like she was at a dead end and didn't know which way to turn. It probably was just an accident, and she didn't need to worry about it anymore. She didn't want to think about anything other than her date. She wanted this feeling to last as long as possible.

CHAPTER 21

Max walked the four blocks to Coast Highway, then turned right. She passed Flower to the People every morning on her way to work, but this morning she knocked on the door to get Eric's attention. She had left for work early knowing he would expect to hear about her date.

Eric unlocked the front door and let her in. The scent of roses and lavender filled the room, and she took a deep breath.

He got right to the point. "So, how was your date?"

"Good morning to you, too," Max said in a teasing voice.

"Fine, good morning. Now tell me. All the details."

"It was fantastic." She gave him a play by play of the evening, leaving out the kiss.

"And was there a goodnight kiss?" When she didn't answer, he said, "I can tell by the look on your face that there was. It must have been a doozy."

“It was really nice,” she answered, smiling at the memory. “Just right for a first kiss.”

“You’re right. It’s too early for tongue.”

“Eric!”

“Was there tongue?”

“No!” She shook her head, then laughed. “It’s definitely too early.”

“Well, if you say so,” he said, looking unconvinced. “Want some coffee?”

“Thanks, but I already had a cup and any more will just make me jittery. Besides, it’s about time for me to get to work. I don’t think even Darlene can ruin my mood today.”

“She usually doesn’t get to you. What’s going on?”

“I wish I knew. She’s been particularly difficult this last week or so.”

"Just more reason to make a go of it on your own. So, are you ready to look at another shop space? Victoria has another for us to look at on Avocado near Fashion Island."

"That location’s got to be expensive," Max said. Fashion Island was just ten miles away, but it held the most exclusive shops and boutiques.

"Just look at it. I've started working on a budget for your shop and you can help me as soon as you're done with the costumes. How about this weekend? The show opens on Friday, right?”

"Yes, and then my job is done. How about Sunday?" Max asked.

Wedding Belles was closed Sundays and Darlene usually gave her Mondays off. She was looking forward to two days of doing absolutely nothing, but it looked like she'd be looking at numbers, which didn't sound fun, but it would give her a better idea if opening her own shop was a good idea financially.

"I'll see if Victoria can show us the space on Sunday, too," Eric said. "I think we're both going to be too busy until then."

Max stared off into space, her thoughts a jumble. Between a death, a stolen ring, the idea of opening her own shop and a first date, she had a lot on her mind.

"Snap out of it!" Eric said.

"What?" Max had almost forgotten he was still standing there. "What are you talking about?"

Eric laughed. "You're in La La Land. You really like this guy, huh?"

"I really do," she admitted.

Wedding Belles was just a block down from Eric's flower shop. Darlene was in her office, as usual, and after calling out a hello, Max went into the workroom to see if there were alterations that needed to be completed. It appeared they were caught up on their work, so she straightened up instead. Darlene let her organize the room the way she wanted, but Darlene never put anything back in the right place. Max was not a neatnik in any sense of the word, but she needed to find things when she was at work, so she tried to maintain order, often feeling like she was fighting a losing battle.

Darlene asked Max to sit in on her 11:00 appointment. Max tried to pay attention during the consultation, but when she went to pull dresses, she wasn't able to zero in on the right dress the way she usually did. She brought five dresses into the Dream Room, which made Darlene smile, but after the bride-to-be had tried on all five, she was sent out to pull more. Max lost count of how many dresses the young woman tried on before she left, saying she'd "think about it."

"What's gotten into you?" Darlene asked. "You're actually doing what I asked you to do for once, and it's not working. Usually, you find the perfect dress right away, but today everything you picked out was a dud."

"I don't know," Max answered. "I feel like I've lost my mojo."

"Well, get it back. That's the first time I can remember in a very long time that you couldn't pick out the right dress." The two of them started gathering up dresses and hanging them back up. "You might as well go to the theater. You're not much use to me today."

Was this the right time to bring up how crummy Darlene's mood had been lately? Max felt too deflated to even start that conversation. She helped Darlene finish cleaning up, and by the time they were done, Keiko had arrived. Max asked if Keiko could come with her to the theater since there was so much still to be done before tomorrow's dress rehearsal, and Darlene reluctantly agreed.

Max was silent on the car ride.

"Why are you so quiet?" Keiko asked. "Did your date not go well?"

"No, the date went great." Max smiled, remembering the evening again. Then her smile faded. "It's just that I seem to have lost my touch."

"Everyone knows that if something is lost, you are the one to find it. So, if anyone can find your lost touch, it is you. But just to be clear, which touch have you lost?"

"We had a bride this morning in to look at wedding gowns, and I couldn't find the right one."

Keiko gasped. "You always find the right one." Keiko pulled the car in to the theater parking lot. "Maybe this is just a one-time thing. Everyone has off days."

"Maybe," Max said glumly. "I'm not so sure. Maybe I've just been lucky."

"No way. You have a talent for seeing things that no one else does. It is your secret power."

"I do think I can figure anything out, even when no one else can. Or at least I used to. Maybe I'm not as smart as I thought I was." She wondered if being in love was affecting her. In love? Wasn't that rushing things a bit? She wasn't even completely sure how she felt about Brian. She wasn't sure about much of anything right now.

"Maybe you're just human," Keiko said. "You know, like the rest of us."

CHAPTER 22

Max wasn't in the mood for sewing. She left Keiko in the costume shop and walked out to the front of the theater to clear her head. The sun felt warm on her face, and she took a deep breath of the sea air. A familiar sight was heading toward her along the sidewalk. It was River, their regular mailman.

River still surfed most mornings before he started his route even though he was no longer a young man. His thinning hair was pulled back into a ponytail.

"Hi, Max," he greeted her. "I haven't seen you around lately."

"I've spent most of my time here at the theater lately helping with costumes."

"Cool." His eyes narrowed as he considered her for a moment. "You look like you have something on your mind."

"River, I think I've lost my mojo." There was something about River that made her confide in him. He always seemed to come up with the right quote from the Dalai Lama or Lao Tse to help her make sense of what was going on in her life. He seemed to have an endless supply of wisdom.

"Nothing is lost, nor ever can be lost. Walt Whitman."

"But I always know just what to do and now I don't."

"I see. That is a completely different problem. But perhaps you do know what to do and you just don't want to do it. Your mojo hasn't gone anywhere. Your ego is not allowing you to hear what it is telling you."

Max stood on the sidewalk, stunned. Was River right? Had she already made up her mind about the people around her and her ego wasn't letting her question herself?

River took several pieces of mail and handed them to Max. "Would you give these to Olivia?"

"Sure, River." He started to walk away but turned back when she called out to him.

"Thank you, River."

"Namaste," he said and continued on his route.

What was her intuition telling her? She needed to look at everything, or rather everyone, fresh. She felt a glimmer of hope. Maybe she could figure out who was to blame in Celeste's death after all.

When Max got back to the costume shop, Keiko was typing at her laptop. "I think we need to get some sewing done," Max hinted. She did some of her best thinking while she was sewing, and she had a lot to think about.

"Instead of catching a jewel thief?" Keiko asked.

"What?" Max walked over to take a look at Keiko's laptop.

There on the screen was an old newspaper article. Max looked at the date and saw it was ten years old. The small headline said, "Peter Nilsson Questioned Re: Jewel Heist."

Max stared at the screen. That was a big coincidence. Was her father's friend a jewel thief? She looked at Keiko who had a sly grin on her face.

"Busted!" Keiko said.

Should they call the police? An article in an old newspaper was hardly proof of anything, but it was quite a coincidence. If he hadn't been arrested, then the police probably wouldn't even know about it.

"So, what are you going to do?" Keiko asked.

"I'm not sure. I think I'd like to talk to Peter again before I go to the police."

"If he stole her ring, do you think he had anything to do with rigging the balcony so Celeste would fall?"

Peter might be a criminal, but did that mean he could be a murderer? It didn't seem that way to Max. "I don't think so. He seemed genuinely distraught over her death." Could that be an act? Max had never been so unsure of herself before.

Max decided to talk with Peter again when he arrived for rehearsal that evening. That should be an interesting conversation.

Max and Keiko were hard at work putting all the finishing touches on the costumes, when Max noticed Keiko staring at her.

"Is something wrong?" Max asked. "Is my hair sticking up or something?"

"No, nothing like that. But something is wrong, I can feel it. You seem like you are miles away."

"I have a lot on my mind, Keiko."

"You mean the murder? And the jewel thief? And not being able to pick out the right wedding gown?"

"Yeah, all that. I always know what to do, but for the first time I can remember, I don't."

"This is just like *Kiki's Delivery Service*!"

"Like what?"

Keiko sighed. "Haven't you watched any of the DVDs I gave you? Kiki is a witch who loses her powers because she loses her confidence."

"So, how does she get her powers back?"

"She needs to find a new purpose. Maybe you need a new purpose."

"I already have a purpose. To find a murderer. Anyway, it's just a movie," Max said.

"Just a movie," Keiko muttered disapprovingly, shaking her head. She started sewing again and the loud hum of the sewing machine drowned out the rest of her mumbling.

Max knew how important those movies were to Keiko, but they were fiction, after all. Still, she felt like she'd hurt her feelings. "As soon as the costumes are done, I'll watch all the movies you gave me." Whether Keiko had heard her or not, she didn't know.

Max continued to sew and think. The one thing she knew she needed to do was to confront Kenneth, but she dreaded the idea. She didn't really think he was a murderer, but he did have a motive if he wanted to keep his gambling and his debts secret from his wife. Then again, was what Peter had told her even true? She thought she knew him, but now she doubted if she could trust anything he said. He might have given her false information to throw her off the trail. Not that she was even sure what trail she was on.

Still, she'd promised herself to look at everyone with fresh eyes. If Kenneth were a murderer, and if he reacted badly to their conversation, Olivia was in the office next to his and would hear her if she screamed.

CHAPTER 23

Max knocked on Kenneth's door and heard him call out, "Come in."

He sat behind his desk and turned away from his computer screen to look at her.

"Is there a problem with the costumes?" he asked.

"No, no problem. I mean, there's a lot of work left to do, but we should be able to get it all done in time for tomorrow's dress rehearsal."

"Tomorrow? Tonight is dress rehearsal. Tonight and tomorrow night."

"Tonight?" Max panicked. "But we're not done!"

"Don't worry about it. We'll use whatever costumes are done or nearly done."

"But I'm not done with the shoes yet."

"Will they be done for tomorrow?"

"Yes, they should be done sometime this evening."

"We'll use the ones that are done for now."

She wasn't sure how many costumes they'd be able to use tonight. There was still so much to do. But costumes weren't what she had come to talk to him about. "There was something else I want to ask you about."

"Yes?" He looked at her with curiosity.

"It's about Celeste," she began. "I know about the gambling and about your debts. And that she threatened to tell Darlene."

Kenneth sighed. "This is just what I was afraid of. Secrets don't stay secret."

"If someone's dead, they can't tell."

"True. Celeste can't tell anyone now. But it doesn't matter anyway. I told Darlene myself the day before Celeste fell. When she died, I thought that if I had only waited one more day that I wouldn't have had to tell her at all. But now I realize it was for the best. It would have come out eventually, and people might have thought I was the murderer." He looked as if a thought had just occurred to him. "Is that why you're here? Because you think I killed her?"

Max laughed nervously. "No, of course not. Hey, is that why Darlene's been in such a bad mood for the past week?"

"You noticed."

"It would be pretty hard not to." Though it didn't seem fair that Darlene was taking out her anger on Max and Keiko.

"When she's in a bad mood, everyone feels it. I had promised her I wouldn't ever gamble again," Kenneth said. "She feels betrayed, and I don't really blame her. I have no way to pay back the money and she's angry about having to bail me out again."

Max was uncomfortable asking her next question. "Were you siphoning money from the theater?"

She didn't know what response she expected, but she certainly didn't expect Kenneth to start crying.

"I planned to pay it back. I had a sure thing that would have paid off my debts, but I needed a few thousand dollars. I thought if I borrowed the money and paid it back a few days later, no one would be the wiser."

"So, is that the real reason the theater has to close?" she asked.

"No. Darlene said she would give me the money I need. But now that George Beidleman has pulled out his funding and Sonia has raised the rent, we can't keep the doors open unless we get new donors or sell out every showing of Romeo and Juliet. Right now, it looks like the theater will be half empty for most of the run."

Max felt better knowing that Kenneth didn't have a motive to harm Celeste, and she was relieved to learn the reason for Darlene's bad mood. Max had been afraid that Darlene was angry with her for some reason. She hoped that Kenneth and Darlene would work things out. They were both flawed, but they were basically good people. Besides, who else would put up with Darlene and her moods? She hoped Darlene would forgive Kenneth and she really hoped Kenneth would be able to kick his gambling habit.

Back at the costume shop, something was still bothering Max, but she couldn't put her finger on it. She and Keiko sewed in silence.

When the last of the shoes was sewn, Max took

them out to the stage. She found Peter in the wings, watching Eric rehearse his sword fight scene and gave him his shoes.

"We need to talk," Max said.

"Okay," Peter said with curiosity in his voice. Max led him back to the costume shop.

"By the way," she tried to segue smoothly, "I know you stole Celeste's ring," she bluffed. Keiko stopped sewing, looking up with interest.

"What are you talking about?" Peter asked.

Max looked for signs of guilt on his face or in his voice but detected none. Still, if he had been a jewel thief, he had to be good at keeping secrets. No wonder her dad said he was such a good poker player.

"Maybe you were afraid you'd be searched last night, so you slipped the ring in my pocket. Or maybe you felt guilty taking a ring off a woman's hand who you thought of like a daughter and had second thoughts." Max hadn't decided if she should tell him she knew that Celeste was his daughter, but at any rate, this was not the time.

Now Peter did a convincing job of looking shocked. But not convincing enough for Max. "What are you saying?" he stammered.

"I know you're a jewel thief. I have proof." It wasn't exactly proof, but it was incriminating. "Tell me the truth, and maybe I won't go to the police."

Peter sighed and looked for a place to sit down, finally settling into the sofa. Max sat down at her sewing machine and waited.

"I managed to never get caught," he began. "I always

planned each theft meticulously, down to the last detail. I considered everything that could go wrong and had a contingency for every possibility. The one time the police questioned me, they couldn't pin a thing on me, and after that I became even more careful. I never acted impulsively. Never. Until that night."

"The night Celeste fell?"

"I checked her pulse and was so relieved that she was alive. It didn't even occur to me that she would die that night. The ring was right there for the taking. A little sleight of hand and it was in my pocket before I even thought about what I was doing. Maybe it had just been so long. It had been hard to quit, but I convinced myself that I had been lucky too long and to keep going would be asking for trouble. I don't even need the money. I just miss the thrill. It's hard to settle down to a quiet retirement when you've lived a life like I have." He hung his head sadly. "Are you going to tell the police?"

"I was just bluffing about having proof." Max knew Peter would never get convicted. And besides, he didn't keep the ring. "The police have more important things to do than to listen to my theories about who took a ring that isn't even missing anymore."

Peter jumped up and hugged her. "It won't happen again. I promise!"

"Now you know I'm on to you, so I'm sure it won't happen again." She thought for a moment. "Maybe you should take hang gliding lessons or something a little more thrilling than bartending."

"Maybe I will. Thanks, Max. I owe you one."

Max followed Peter back to the stage so she could give Eric his shoes. She looked around the theater hoping to see Brian. He was talking to Heather, both of them looking very serious. He looked up and saw her watching him. His face lit up in a big grin and he gave her a little wave. Max smiled back, thinking about how lucky she was to have someone like Brian interested in her.

Eric and the man she now knew as Zach were rehearsing their fight scene and she was impressed with how naturally Eric wielded his fake sword. She'd barely noticed Zach before, and on a hunch, looked around the wings of the stage. Sure enough, Olivia was watching the scene with a dopey smile on her face. Yep, she was in love, or on the fast track to it for sure. Kenneth stopped the two actors twice to correct the choreography. When they finally got to the end of the scene, Max walked out onto the stage to give Eric his shoes.

"Hi, Zach," she said to the other actor. "I don't think we've actually met. I'm Max."

"Olivia's told me all about you. It's nice to meet you." Max liked his warm smile and the way his face seemed to light up when he said Olivia's name.

Zach stood at least six feet tall with thick blonde hair combed straight back that looked like it might fall into his eyes at any moment. He wore straight-legged jeans and a loose long sleeved black t-shirt that didn't hide his fit body. Max could certainly understand why Olivia was attracted to him. She found herself hoping Olivia had finally found love. She suppressed the desire to have Keiko do a background check on him.

Kenneth complimented her on how realistic the faux leather shoes looked.

Max looked up to see a small, dark-haired man walking up the center aisle. It was Ivan! She took out her phone and texted Detective Cruz.

Kenneth's back was to the audience, and when he noticed that everyone had stopped talking, he turned around to see what they were all looking at.

"Ivan! Where have you been?" Max couldn't tell if Kenneth's tone of voice denoted concern or irritation.

"I have seen lawyer," he said. "Immigration lawyer. I should have done it long ago, but I was afraid to be deported."

"Deported?" Kenneth asked. "Are you here illegally?"

"I come here twenty years ago on a tourist visa. I got fake passport, and all was fine until a few months ago when they take me into custody. They make mistake and let me out, so I come here. I think no one will look for me here. Then I see police car in front of theater. I don't know what to do, so I hide."

Another piece of the mystery, but it didn't get her any closer to solving Celeste's murder. Unless Celeste knew he was here illegally and threatened to turn him in. But how would she have known that? Max pondered the idea, but the fact that he had returned made it seem unlikely that he was guilty.

"Now I have lawyer, and I can stay and work until I have hearing." Ivan looked at the stage, noticing the actors for the first time. "What is on their feet?" he cried out.

"They delivered the wrong shoes, and the right ones were going to take two weeks to arrive," Kenneth explained. "Max made shoes for all the actors. I think they will do quite well."

"No, no, no!" Ivan seemed beside himself. "This will never do. I leave you alone for a few days and you ruin everything."

"Listen here." Max surprised herself by speaking up. "Keiko and I have worked our butts off making these shoes, and if it weren't for us, all of your actors would be barefoot or wearing sneakers. So, I don't want to hear another word about it."

Ivan just stared at her. "Who are you?"

"I'm Max. Remember? Not short for anything. Just Max."

Someone was clapping out in the audience. Max peered out into the darkness and saw Detective Cruz walking up the aisle.

"I'd listen to her if I were you. She's not someone you want to cross. By the way, I have some questions for you, Ivan. If that's your real name."

"Yes, Ivan is my real name. Ivan Sokolov. And if you are going to ask questions, I want my lawyer."

"That can be arranged," the detective agreed.

Max glanced over at where Brian stood grinning. He gave her a thumbs up.

"Everyone back to work," Kenneth barked out, and Max slipped away.

"So, he actually clapped?" Keiko asked when Max was back in the costume shop.

"You should have been there," Fiona said excitedly. "Max was a force to be reckoned with. 'I've worked my ass off making these shoes.'"

"I'm pretty sure I didn't say ass."

"Fine. Butt. The point is, she put Ivan in his place, and Detective Cruz heard the whole thing and told Ivan he should do what she told him."

"I wish I had seen it for myself," Keiko said. "So, is Ivan back as the director?"

"I don't know," Fiona said. "Kenneth may want to cut his losses and stay as director for the run of the show. Most of the director's work is done by this point in the production anyway."

"Then we won't get to see what Ivan thinks of the blue dress," Keiko said. "If he had that reaction over the shoes, the blue dress might send him over the edge."

"True dat," Fiona said, and Max and Keiko laughed. "By the way, have you seen Josie around?"

"No, I haven't seen her all evening. I thought you might have left her at home."

"I put her down on the stage when I arrived, and she snuck off. I know you girls are busy, but would you mind helping me look for her? Teresa would kill me if anything happened to that cat."

Max and Keiko didn't need much of an excuse to take a break from all their sewing, so they helped Fiona search for Josie backstage, looking in the offices and dressing rooms with no luck. Finally, Keiko called out,

"Found her!" and Fiona and Max headed toward her voice.

Keiko was underneath the balcony set where there was barely room to crawl but plenty of room for a cat.

"You get her," Fiona said to Max. "She likes you better than me."

Max crouched down on her hands and knees and crept in the narrow space under the balcony. Josie was swatting something around. Could it be? It was! She was playing with a metal nut. She reached for Josie and pulled her out from under the set, Josie protesting with a yowl.

Max texted Detective Cruz and stood guard while she waited for him to arrive.

"What if there are fingerprints on the nut? That could solve the case," Keiko said happily.

"It would mean the murderer isn't very smart," Max said. "Which is possible, but not likely. They'd have to be a fool not to wear gloves or wipe off their prints."

"But what if the nut fell off the balcony and the killer couldn't find it, so he didn't get the chance to wipe off his prints."

"His or her prints," Max corrected. "That's an interesting theory. I like it. But come to think of it, if they used a wrench, there probably wouldn't be prints."

"Well, I've got to get back to rehearsal," Fiona said. "Let me know if you learn anything."

"I'll be in the costume shop," Keiko said. Max wondered if they were leaving her to meet with the detective alone on purpose, but she didn't give it much thought. She was glad she would get a chance to talk with him without other ears listening in.

Detective Cruz finally arrived to retrieve the nut. Max was surprised to find that her heart still did a little somersault when she saw him. She thought after her date with Brian that she'd be over her crush on the handsome detective.

"How'd you find it? The CSI did a thorough search."

"Josie found it," Max said. "She was playing with it, so you may find paw prints on it. Hopefully, she didn't mess up any fingerprints, if any were left on it."

"Maybe I should take her paw prints so I can exclude them."

Max looked at him. It was the first time she remembered him making a joke. He wasn't smiling, but it had to be a joke, right?

"Just kidding," he said.

"I knew that." So, he had a dry sense of humor. At least he had a sense of humor. She learned more about Detective Cruz every day that made her like him better. She felt a bit guilty but told herself she couldn't be the first woman who had a crush on two men at the same time.

Max went back to the costume shop and found Keiko on her laptop.

"What are you doing on your computer? We have a lot of sewing to get done." Max said.

"I just wanted to do some more research. If you're going to be dating Brian, I wanted to know more about him."

"Keiko! Are you really doing a background check on my new boyfriend?"

"Oh, so he is your boyfriend now. I was just checking out his Facebook page. And by that, I mean all of his friends' Facebook pages. When I get started, I can't stop."

"Well, please make yourself stop. I don't want you prying."

"So, you don't want to see the pictures of him skydiving?" She turned her laptop around and showed a picture of Brian with a parachute on his back. "I remember you said he was afraid of heights."

Max stared at the picture. What did it mean? He told Ivan he was afraid to climb up the side of the balcony, but he went skydiving? If he lied about his fear of heights, what else had he lied about?

Max and Keiko went back to work on the costumes, Max lost in her own thoughts and Keiko quietly working at one of the sewing machines.

Max sent Keiko home around nine while she kept sewing. Olivia had offered to give Max a ride home when they were done rehearsing but didn't know how late it would be.

Brian poked his head in the open door.

"Still working?" he asked rhetorically.

"There's still a lot to be done. Didn't you notice the missing costumes during your rehearsal?"

Max kept sewing on the machine, not wanting to confront Brian, but knowing she needed to. He watched her work for a few minutes and then turned to go.

"Wait," Max said before he got to the door. "Can we talk?"

"That doesn't sound good. Especially after only one date. You're not breaking up with me already, are you? I haven't even had a chance to tell you my most boring stories or subjected you to my worst puns. Did you know I love puns? You don't know what you're missing."

"No, it's nothing like that. Keiko just found something online. I can't keep her off the computer."

"She was checking up on me?"

"I had no idea," she quickly explained. "She did it without telling me."

"No problem. I don't have any secrets. What did she find?"

"You went skydiving," she said, "but you told me you were afraid of heights."

Brian sighed and plopped down on the sofa. "I hate weakness, especially in myself. I hate that I'm afraid of heights. I thought if I went skydiving, it would help me get over it. I mean, after that, what could scare me? I'm completely embarrassed to tell you this, but I couldn't go through with it. I had a panic attack on the plane—I couldn't even get near the door. I cowered in the back of the plane until we landed."

"I'm sorry," Max said. "I didn't mean to pry." Was he telling her the truth? She wanted to believe him, but how well did she really know him? If she let her feelings get in the way, she was never going to solve this case. But Brian was such a sweet guy, he couldn't possibly hurt anyone, could he?

"That's okay. I'm kind of glad you know. I don't want to keep any secrets from you. It's late. Can I give you a ride home?"

"Thanks," she said, forcing a smile, "but Olivia's giving me a ride."

Detective Cruz entered and said hello to both of them, though he seemed especially cold to Brian. Brian said goodnight and gave her a kiss on the lips. Max felt awkward and avoided looking at either of them. She wasn't sure what she was feeling, but she wished Brian hadn't kissed her in front of the detective.

Max started packing up to go home, waiting for the detective to tell her what he was doing back at the theater.

He asked her to take a walk with him. Max slipped on her sweater, and they went around to the back of the theater, past the patio and walked across the lawn toward the cliff. The waves below glowed in the moonlight and the sound of them crashing on the shore made her shoulders start to relax. It had been a very long day.

"I know you like your tea," he said, handing her a paper cup with a lid. "It's English Breakfast. I hope that's okay."

"That's great, thanks." He was thoughtful, too. Why was she just now noticing all his great qualities? She tried not to think about it, which was hard with him standing close to her.

Maybe a little caffeine would help perk her up. She knew, as tired as she was, that it wouldn't keep her from being able to fall asleep tonight. She took a sip.

He'd even put just the right amount of sugar in it. "So," Max finally asked what she was dying to know. "Were there any fingerprints on the nut?"

"Yes." He paused for effect. "Peter's."

"Peter's?" Max thought for a moment. "Well, he helped build the set, so that's not surprising."

"Do actors usually help build sets?"

"Oh, sure. I don't think it's mandatory, but most of them help out, especially in a community theater like this one. Olivia tells me there's something everyone can do, even if it's just painting."

"Then the fingerprint is meaningless." He sounded disappointed.

"It does tell us the murderer must have worn gloves. Or they used a wrench or pliers."

Olivia came looking for her and turned to leave when she saw them.

"Olivia," Max said, "are you ready to go?"

Olivia looked sheepish, as if she'd interrupted something. "I can wait, if you're talking."

Detective Cruz told her to go home and get some rest. Was there more he wanted to say? She'd have to wait to find out.

CHAPTER 24

Wednesday morning Max and Keiko were going straight to the theater with Darlene's grudging approval since they needed to have all the costumes completed for the final dress rehearsal that night. Keiko came over to Richard's house to pick her up.

"Oatmeal?" Richard asked. "You're going to need your strength to get through the day. It sounds like it's going to be a long one."

"Thanks," Keiko said, and sat down at the table with Max. "I did some research on George's company," she told Max. "It looks like they were in some real financial trouble."

"Really. That's interesting information. Would a million dollars have saved the business?"

"Definitely. They're behind on the rent and haven't paid their subcontractors. A million dollars would put them back in business and then some."

"And when you consider he thought she was having an affair with Brian, it sounds like a motive to me."

"Brian?" Richard asked. "Is this the same Brian you went on a date with?"

"Yes, it's the same one," Max said. "And no, he wasn't having an affair with Celeste."

"Are you sure?" he asked. "Are you just taking his word for it?"

Max frowned. She tried to remember what everyone else had said. No one had any actual proof he was having an affair, but a lot of people seemed to think he was. Was she letting her personal feelings interfere with her normally logical thinking?

"I've thought about how I would feel if he did have an affair with Celeste. On one hand, it doesn't have anything to do with me, but it does say something about his character if he had an affair with a married woman. I think the worst part would be if he lied to me about it. I have a lot of trouble forgiving people, especially if they've lied to me."

"I could never lie to you, even if I wanted to," Keiko said. "You would see right through me."

"Me, too," said Richard.

"Well, my radar is a bit off lately," Max said. "I feel like I'm letting my emotions get the better of me, and it's affecting my judgment."

Max and Keiko had just gotten into Keiko's car when Max got a text from Darlene saying she wanted to see her right away. What could that be about?

Keiko, who always avoided anything that hinted of confrontation, waited in the car while Max went into the shop to see Darlene. Darlene came out of her office with her arms folded over her chest.

"So, when were you going to tell me?" Darlene demanded.

"Tell you what?" Max's voice was barely more than a squeak.

"You're opening your own bridal shop! After everything I've done for you?"

Max didn't know how to reply. After everything she'd done for her? Max had been a loyal employee for years. She'd never promised Darlene anything. In spite of that, she felt guilty.

“What do you mean, after everything you’ve done for me? What about what I’ve done for you? I’ve practically run the store for you this past year. You just sit in that office working on the computer.”

“Running a bridal shop isn’t just helping brides pick out their wedding gowns. While you’re sewing, I’m dealing with the business side of things, something you know nothing about.”

“Well, I can learn.”

“I don't know why I care. You’ll be out of business in six months and then you’ll come crawling back to me looking to get your old job back.”

“I’ll never come back. You’re the most difficult person I’ve ever had to work for.” Even her boss in New York wasn’t as demanding as Darlene.

“We’ll see,” Darlene said, a smug look on her face.

Max tried to keep her anger in check, but she felt it simmering inside her, ready to explode. There were so many things she wanted to say, but she was afraid she’d regret it later. She finally told Darlene, “I haven't made a decision yet."

"Well, I'll make it for you. You're fired."

"Fired?" Max stood there with her mouth half open. She'd just been fired for the first time in her life. Her self-control had reached its limit. “You can’t fire me. I quit!”

“Fine, go ahead and quit. And there’s no need to give me notice. I accept your resignation, effective immediately.”

Max was about to storm out when she remembered the unfinished costumes. "What about the theater?"

"That's between you and Kenneth."

Yeah, but Kenneth was her husband. If Darlene told Kenneth to fire her, too, she'd go from having two jobs to none in a day. But Kenneth needed her, if only for a few more days.

Keiko must have realized something terrible had happened by the look on Max’s face when she got back in the car. She asked Max what was wrong but got no response. Max just stared out the window. Keiko grabbed Max's purse and dug down until she found what she was looking for--her emergency dark chocolate. She unwrapped it and handed it to Max who dutifully put it in her mouth and let it melt on her tongue.

"Okay, now tell me what happened in there," Keiko said.

"She fired me," Max said quietly and calmly. “And then I quit.” She felt completely numb.

"She fired you?” Keiko's voice was incredulous. “You

wait right here. I'm going in to give that woman a piece of my mind and quit, too."

"Wait," Max reached out to stop Keiko, "don’t do anything right away. It's good to let things sink in before you do anything."

"I don't want to let things sink in. I want to quit right now."

"One of us needs to have a job until I open my new shop."

Keiko squealed. "Is that why she fired you? I can't believe you didn't tell me. You're going to hire me, right? What am I saying, of course you are. When did all this happen? Never mind, we can talk about all this later. Where do you want to go now? Do you want to drown your sorrows or celebrate?” She paused as if she had run out of steam. “I'm so confused."

Max had never heard Keiko say so much at one time, and she started to laugh. Then Keiko started laughing and they kept laughing until Max started to cry. The tears streamed down her face, and she knew she was ruining her makeup, but she didn't care. She wasn't even sure why she was crying. She took the tissues Keiko handed her and blew her nose. Finally, she was cried out and took a deep breath. When one door closes, another opens. Wasn't that the way the saying went? In a way, it had gone the other way around. One door opened, then another closed. What did she want to do right now?

"I want to finish the costumes," Max told Keiko.

"Really?"

"I need to talk to Kenneth first and see if Darlene's

told him to fire me, too. But that would be really stupid of him, since we're not done with the costumes and opening night is two days away."

"Okay, if you say so."

Keiko drove to the theater and waited in the costume shop while Max went to see Kenneth. He begged her to stay and even offered to talk to his wife about giving Max her job back, but Max told him not to bother. She walked down the hall past Olivia's office. She didn't want to talk to her yet.

Max sat on the sofa and watched Keiko sew. She felt completely drained of energy.

"Do you need more chocolate?" Keiko asked.

"No, I need to get to work." No matter how she felt, she had a responsibility to get the costumes done before the show opened.

“Are you sure you want to sew?” Keiko asked. “I can get most of the work done by myself. Why don’t you just relax?”

Max sighed. “When I was a little girl and I had no one to play with, I would spend hours in my room sewing clothes for my dolls. When one of the girls in the neighborhood finally came over to play, she thought I had the best-dressed Barbies of anyone. All the kids had to come over just to see them, then they started asking me to sew clothes for their dolls. I became almost popular. All because of sewing. Sewing always makes me happy, so that's what I need to do right now."

Max and Keiko sewed nonstop, only taking a break when Olivia brought them sandwiches for lunch.

Olivia could tell right away that something was wrong, and Max told her that Darlene had fired her.

"How dare she! What possible reason did she give you?"

"I guess there's no harm in telling you now. Eric has offered to help me open my own bridal shop. I guess I was fooling myself to think that anything like that could stay secret in this town."

Olivia gave her a hug before she left and told Max to come see her if she needed to talk.

Before Max got back to work, she went to pull her notebook out of her tote bag but remembered it had gone missing. Notebook or not, there was still a murder to solve. She found some paper in a drawer, and Keiko helped her recreate her suspect list.

Looking at all the names on the list, the only one who had a motive and opportunity was George Beidleman. But how could she actually prove it? Should she confront him? She remembered the last time she'd confronted a murderer and decided against it. Sometimes the best way to come up with a solution was to quit thinking about a problem, so she went back to sewing.

The costumes were mostly done by six o'clock when the actors started arriving, with just a few pins holding up some of the hems. There was a flurry of activity as they all came in to get their costumes for the first act.

Friends and family had been invited to watch the final dress rehearsal, and Max and Keiko decided to sit in the audience with the thirty or so other people who had come to see the play for free. Max wanted to see Eric's sword fight scene. She watched Eric, as Mercutio, cross swords with Tybalt, until Tybalt killed Mercutio. Eric collapsed, then tried to rise, then collapsed again, repeated the process and finally died with a loud cry of anguish. Then Romeo, who had been trying to stop the two from fighting, stabbed Tybalt. Zach died much quicker than Eric had.

Everyone clapped, and Max took the opportunity to slip out of the theater and back to the costume shop in case any of the actors needed her assistance. When she entered, Josie was giving her a look as if to say, "where have you been?"

Max sat down on the sofa and Josie curled up on her lap and started purring. What was it about a warm cat on your lap that could make you feel like things weren't so bad? She scratched behind the cat's ears and smiled as the purring got louder.

Eric stopped in to visit since he didn't have any more scenes in the play. He plopped down on the sofa next to her.

"So, what did you think?" he asked.

"Your sword fighting was very realistic," she said. "I was very impressed."

"And what about my acting?" He waited expectantly for her answer.

Max thought about how to say it diplomatically. "You were very… well, I mean, I really could tell your death was very painful."

He narrowed his eyes. "Are you saying I overdid it?"

"No! No, of course not. I assume that being stabbed

to death would hurt a lot, and you portrayed that very well."

"Okay," he said, but she wasn't sure he was convinced. "I'm not a professional actor. Besides, you were probably watching Brian the whole time."

"That's not true. Anyway, your sword fighting was better than anyone's. Including Brian's."

"At least I have that much going for me. Speaking of Brian, has he asked you on another date?"

"He said he wants to see me again." She hadn't really thought about a second date, and it was the farthest thing from her mind right now. "I don't know when. He's very busy with the play."

"What's wrong? You don't seem like yourself."

"I've been fired."

"What?" Eric's voice went up an octave. "Darlene fired you?"

"This morning. She was angry about me starting my own shop, although I told her I hadn't made the decision yet."

"Looks like she made it for you," Eric said.

"I'm not going to make such a big decision because I got fired. I still need time to decide if it's the right thing for me to do." Madam Giana said that she would leave something or someone. Did she mean Max would leave Crystal Shores? Maybe getting fired was a sign she should go back to New York, but just the thought of leaving her dad and all her friends made her wistful.

Eric sighed. "Fine," he said, sounding disappointed. "Take your time."

"Thanks."

"Now, let's get back to the subject of your dating life. I'm glad to see you dating again. I hope it means you're over Andy."

Andy was her childhood friend who she had been in love with for years, but who didn't return her feelings. "I've been over him for a while. I just hadn't met anyone I wanted to go out with."

"And you're sure Brian didn't kill Celeste?"

"Eric!"

He just laughed. "I figured you wouldn't be dating him if you thought he was a suspect. Do you still think it wasn't an accident?"

"I'm sure now it wasn't an accident. That's what my gut told me from the beginning. I just wish it would tell me who was guilty."

"If it were only that easy!"

Eric gave her a long, warm hug and then stood up to go. "Everything's going to be okay. I promise you."

Max didn't want to disturb the cat on her lap, so she stayed on the sofa. She hoped Eric was right and everything would be okay.

Without warning, Josie jumped from Max's lap. Before she knew it, Josie had a little grey mouse trapped under one of her paws. Max closed her eyes, not wanting to see what happened next, but then her curiosity got the better of her and she opened one eye.

Josie and the mouse were nose to nose, both of their whiskers twitching. It appeared as if they were having a serious conversation. Then the mouse seemed to nod, almost imperceptibly. Max blinked. She was so tired her eyes were playing tricks on her. Then Josie lifted her paw, and the mouse scampered away.

Had Josie and the mouse come to some sort of understanding? Max shook her head. Her imagination was really getting the best of her. Still, she was glad that Josie hadn't harmed the mouse. She knew mice could cause all kinds of havoc in the theater, chewing wires and leaving droppings, but they were just so darn cute. If Josie had decided to scare them off instead of killing them, she was fine with that.

"Did you make a new friend, Josie?" She asked the cat who sat licking her fur. "I guess that mouse knows who's boss." Josie stared at her with a bored look.

Josie decided to scare them, not kill them. Was that what someone meant to do to Celeste? Scare her? It made sense in a way, but Max couldn't quite put the pieces together.

At intermission, Heather came in complaining that her corset wasn't tight enough. Max pulled the cords as tight as she felt she could and still allow Heather to breathe. Other actors stopped in between scenes to make fixes or just to visit. Fiona, of course, was one who wanted to chat.

"Eric told me what happened," Fiona said, giving her a hug. "Do you want me to talk to Darlene? I have no problem telling her off."

"Thanks, Fiona," Max said, "but I'd rather handle it on my own. I'm a grown woman, after all."

"Sorry. Sometimes I forget. Part of me still thinks of you as an adorable little tomboy. Still, if you change your mind, you just let me know. Darlene and I go way back, you know."

Max was all alone at last relaxing on the sofa when she had an unexpected visitor: Darlene. She really didn't want to talk to her right now, but she invited her in.

Darlene pulled up a chair and sat directly across from her but said nothing. Max told herself to stay calm.

"Are you here for a reason?" Max finally asked.

"Yes," Darlene said. "I've come to apologize. I hate to admit it, but I overreacted."

"Thank you," Max said, but it would take more than that to convince her to forgive Darlene.

"I have always thought of you as a daughter." Darlene paused and frowned. "I see that look on your face. There was a reason I never had children. I would have been a terrible mother. I know I'm too critical and I only give praise when I think it's warranted, which is rarely."

Max didn't know what to say so she said nothing, but everything Darlene said was true.

"But you deserve praise," Darlene continued. "You have a gift. It's a gift I never had. I bought the bridal shop because it was a profitable business, and it has continued to be. But a good part of the reason it's been profitable is because of you. When you were in New York, our sales suffered. I didn't know what dresses I should order without you there. And women kept calling in asking for you. You have developed quite a reputation. You should be very proud of yourself."

Max was stunned. Darlene had never said these things to her before, and she hadn't realized how much Darlene's praise would mean to her until this moment. She didn't know what to say, so she just nodded, waiting for Darlene to get to the point, if she had one.

"When I found out you were opening your own shop, I didn't want to lose you again, but instead of telling you that, I reacted out of hurt. Like I said, I think of you like a daughter, but I realize you never thought of me like a mother, even after you lost yours. If you did, you would have told me you were thinking of opening your own shop."

"I didn't know how you'd react. I figured I'd wait until I made up my mind. Why stir up trouble if I decided not to go through with it?"

"I realize that now. You don't tell your employer you might quit before you're ready. And I realized that I'm just your employer."

"That's not true, Darlene. You're my mentor. You taught me everything I know about the bridal business. You took me under your wing when I was just a teenager and let me help design dresses with you when I was just out of high school." She thought about the right thing to say, although why she was concerned about Darlene's feelings after what happened, she wasn't sure. "It's true, you're not like a mother to me. You're more like an aunt. A strict but caring aunt who wants the best for me."

Darlene smiled and reached over to pat Max on the knee. For Darlene, that was about as affectionate as she got. Max couldn't remember a single time she'd hugged her. “An aunt. I’ll take that.” She looked thoughtful, and Max waited for her to continue. “I wanted to offer you your job back until you open your shop.”

That was a relief, but Max didn’t want to seem too eager. “I’ll have to sleep on it.”

“I can teach you some more things you need to know, like dealing with suppliers, and I can help you work up a business plan and a budget.”

“You’d do that for me?” Max wasn’t sure what to think.

“Go ahead and sleep on it, and we’ll talk tomorrow. Can you come in at ten?”

“Sure, I suppose so,” Max said.

After Darlene left, Max thought about what Darlene had said. She’d always known that Darlene cared about her in her own way, but this was the first time in ten years she’d ever expressed it in words. Max already knew she would accept her offer. Having Darlene’s help would improve her odds greatly for making her own shop a success. But she was surprised at the relief she felt that there wouldn’t be bad blood between them. At that moment, she made up her mind and grinned. She was going to open up her own bridal shop!

She texted Keiko to say she had her job back and let her know she’d be a little later to the theater tomorrow. Keiko responded in various emoticons, which Max took to mean she was happy about the news.

Max heard a noise and looked up. There was Evelyn with her tray and two cups of tea. She said something in her quiet, hoarse voice, which Max couldn’t hear.

"Excuse me?" Max said, leaning closer to the old woman.

"I brought you tea and cookies. Did you like the snickerdoodles?"

Max didn't know what to say, so she just gave her a sheepish look.

"Never mind," Evelyn said. "My grandson loves them, so I'll leave the cookies here in case he stops by."

She placed the tray on the table and shuffled out the door.

It took a moment for her words to sink in. "Wait," Max called after her. "Your grandson?"

Evelyn didn't answer. Max went to the door and looked down the hall in both directions, but she was gone. She walked to the kitchen at the back of the theater, then retraced her steps and headed the other direction out to the side of the theater. She got there just in time to see Evelyn getting into a car. She stood and watched it drive away, smiling to herself. That woman was growing on her.

CHAPTER 25

Max woke up the next morning feeling happy. Sure, a murderer might be running around loose, but she'd caught a jewel thief, got her job back, was going to open her own bridal shop with Eric and Darlene's support, and she even had a potential boyfriend. Now, if she could just get George Beidleman to confess to murder, her day would be perfect.

But something didn't fit. George had a motive to kill Celeste—money—but no motive that she could see to injure her. And Celeste shouldn't have died from a ten-foot fall. It was just a fluke that she broke her neck.

She got out her notes again and read through the names on her list. No one else made sense. It had to be George. Or did it?

She knew better than to adjust the facts to fit a theory, but that's just what she was doing. If George didn't have a motive to harm Celeste, then she had to admit he didn't have a motive. That meant she had no one left who could have killed Celeste. Unless Detective Cruz had learned something she didn't know, it looked like the case would remain closed.

Over oatmeal, Max told Richard about getting fired and rehired and about Darlene's offer to help her.

"Well, that was a change of heart," Richard said, "but I always knew she had a soft spot for you."

"Really? How could you tell? All she does is bark at me."

"Look at how many people she's hired and fired," he said. "No one meets her standards. No one except you."

"And Keiko." Keiko was the best assistant they'd had in ten years.

"Yes, but you hired Keiko. I think Darlene keeps her around to make you happy."

"Plus, she's very talented," she added.

"She's fired plenty of talented people," he reminded her. "She even fired you, even if she did take it back." Richard got up and poured himself a second cup of coffee. With his back to her, he said, "I don't know if I told you how proud I am of you."

"Thanks, Dad." She knew he was getting choked up, so she chatted about her plans for the new shop while he gained his composure. After a minute, he sat back down at the table.

"You sound excited," he said. "I was afraid you were in a bit of a rut and might decide to move back to New York."

"I knew I wanted to stay here, but you're right. I have been in a bit of a rut. I'm ready for a new challenge. And this is a doozy!"

"Let me know how your meeting with Darlene goes," he said. "Speaking of that, don't you need to get going?"

"Oh no! It wouldn't do to be late today, of all days!" Max said and rushed out the door.

Darlene's mood was greatly improved from the way she'd been acting for the past week.

"I found my original business plan that I made when I opened Wedding Belles, so I made you a copy. There are probably templates online to make it easier these days, but I thought it might help you to see what I did."

The two women chatted for an hour, and Darlene seemed to enjoy talking about when she opened the shop.

"I don't want to mislead you in any way," Darlene said. "It's a lot of work."

"Well, I survived this past week, so I feel like I'm ready." She'd never worked so many hours. "I really appreciate you helping me."

"And I appreciate you not opening your shop in the same town. Hopefully, you won't steal away too much business from me."

"You're an institution," Max said, and then realized that came out wrong. "I mean—"

"I know what you mean. And it's okay. At my age, I don't mind being called an institution. There are worse things to be called."

"Like tough old broad?" Max said and laughed at Darlene's concerned look. "Fiona says she's earned the title," she explained.

“Maybe I’ll feel that way when I’m her age. I'm still not sure if I should be offended when I’m offered a senior discount without asking.”

Max agreed to come back to work until she was ready to open her shop. But first, there was one more day at the theater, so she thanked Darlene for the advice and left. She stepped outside and remembered she didn't have a way to get to the theater. The sun shone in a clear blue sky and Max decided to walk, since she'd been sitting so much lately. Chez Mer was on the way, so she called and ordered two French Dip sandwiches, which were ready by the time she got there. She arrived at the theater shortly before noon feeling like all the cobwebs were cleared from her head, and very hungry.

Keiko had beat her to the theater and looked up when she walked in. "Is that lunch?" she asked. "You spoil me."

"If you think I spoil you already, wait until you taste this sandwich."

Max and Keiko cleared room on the table so they could eat their lunch. The tray that Evelyn had brought was still there.

“I see that old lady brought us more cookies,” Keiko said.

“I found out her name is Evelyn. She said her grandson would eat them. You don’t suppose she’s Brian’s grandmother, do you?” Max surmised.

“Maybe. That would explain why she's been hanging around the theater. Maybe she just wants to be close to him. You should ask him about her the next time you see him. She seems sweet. And her tea is delicious."

"Too bad her cookies are so terrible. Although I'm just judging by the first one I ate. I haven't been brave enough to try any of the others she's brought."

Tonight was preview night. The theater offered discount tickets for those who wanted to see the play without paying full price. That meant that all the costumes needed to be done, although no one would probably notice if a few hems were held up by pins.

Max read aloud from the list she'd made the night before of the work that still needed to be done. Most of the costumes merely needed finishing touches, and there were the alterations on Eric's costume to finish, but Max was having trouble focusing on sewing.

"What about the rest of Heather's dresses?" Keiko asked. "Do they need to be taken in, too?"

Max had completely forgotten about Heather's other costumes. She was two sizes smaller than Celeste. "Well, the nightgown is fine. That's all loose and billowy. If we can't get to the other two dresses by tonight, I'll use safety pins so they don't look baggy on her. I might have to finish them tomorrow."

Even though Max knew they should be focusing on sewing today, she couldn't get her mind off the murder. She told Keiko she had decided that George Beidleman didn't make a good suspect after all and explained how she'd come to that conclusion.

"Then who is left on your list?" Keiko asked.

"No one," Max admitted. "No one who could have

removed the nut and also had a motive to harm Celeste."

"Maybe it was an unfortunate accident," Keiko said. "I know you don't want to think so, but it is a possibility."

"It's not that I don't want to think so. I'd be happy to think that no one is to blame for what happened to Celeste. But unless someone makes a mistake, it looks like the case is going to stay closed."

"We could do some more research," Keiko suggested, reaching for her laptop.

"What we need to do today is sew," Max said. "Tonight is the preview and opening night is tomorrow, so we have just about run out of time. I think I should finish the alterations on Eric's costume, so he doesn't have to have pins sticking out of him tonight."

"He did seem a bit annoyed about having to sword fight while trying not to poke himself." Keiko put her laptop back in its case and reached for one of the unfinished dresses instead.

"Then it's settled. If he's going to be my financial backer, I want to stay on his good side. I'll get to work on it."

"By the way," Keiko asked. "How did the meeting with Darlene go?"

"Really good," Max said, and filled her in on the details.

"So, you are going to open up your own bridal shop?" Keiko looked at her expectantly.

"I am," Max said.

Keiko squealed and jumped up to hug her. "And you're hiring me, of course."

"Of course," Max said. "I wouldn't want to do it without you." Max planned to give Keiko a partial ownership of the shop, but she wanted to talk to Eric first before she said anything. Besides all of her talents, Keiko made coming to work fun. Max hoped they would be working together for a long, long time.

CHAPTER 26

By mid-afternoon, Max decided it was time for a break. Tea sounded really good, so she went down the hall toward the kitchen. She knocked at Olivia's door to find out if she'd like a cup of tea also.

"Come in," Olivia called out.

"I was heading for the kitchen to make us some tea. Would you like some?" Max asked.

Olivia looked up from her computer and indicated a large to-go cup. "Triple expresso over ice. At this point in the rehearsal process, I'm running on pure caffeine."

"Is it always this hectic?"

"Sometimes it's worse! Actors quit, tech people don't show up for work, all kinds of things can go wrong. This is the first time we've had an actor die, though. It may sound cold, but we can replace one actor."

"It just sounds realistic. You're trying to put on a play in spite of all the crazy stuff going on."

"You mean like Celeste's ring being stolen?" Olivia asked. "That was pretty crazy. Did the police figure out who took it?"

"No, they didn't." Max didn't like keeping secrets from her friend, but she had made a promise to Peter. "The ring turned up, so I don't think they're focusing on finding who took it."

"I guess not. How are the costumes coming? You do know tonight is the preview."

Max laughed. "Yes, I know. I'm not that scatter-brained. We're almost done. We would have been done a long time ago if we didn't have to make one whole new dress for Heather and shoes for everyone."

"You've done an amazing job."

"Thanks," Max said and turned to go, and then remembered what she'd been meaning to ask Olivia for days. "By the way, who is this Evelyn who keeps bringing us tea?"

"Evelyn?" Olivia looked thoughtful. "I don't know anyone by that name."

"Odd. She said her grandson was here. I thought maybe she was Brian's grandmother. She's gotta be at least in her eighties and doesn't move that fast. You must have seen her. She walks around with a tea service and gourmet teas." How could someone wander around the theater without anyone else noticing?

"Then she knows her way around our kitchen. I hardly ever go in there, but there is a lovely tray and teapot. I don't know where she got the tea, though. All we have is the cheap stuff."

"Very mysterious," Max said. The next time the old

woman stopped by, Max decided she would find out who she was and what she was doing at the theater.

"I know!" Olivia said with a twinkle in her eye. "Maybe she was the ghost that Heather saw."

"Very funny," Max said. "I know she's real. Keiko saw her, too." Then she remembered that Evelyn was there shortly before Heather thought she saw a ghost. Maybe Evelyn had walked behind the theater and Heather saw her through the fog. Another thing to ask the next time she saw her.

Max returned to the costume shop with tea for Keiko and herself. The only tea she found in the kitchen was orange pekoe, which wasn't anything like the tea that Evelyn brought them, but it would have to do.

Max grabbed the notes out of her tote and stared at her list of suspects. She couldn't stop thinking she was missing something. What if someone wasn't telling the truth?

There was Brian, of course, who said he was afraid of heights. Was she letting her feelings get in the way of her judgment? His motive would be revenge, but ten years was a long time to wait to get back at someone.

Heather had carpel tunnel syndrome, but could she have loosened a nut? It seemed unlikely if she couldn't even open a bottle of water that Max opened easily. She had a good motive to hurt Celeste if she wanted the part of Juliet badly enough. Was it possible that a part could be that important? After all, it was just a community theater. It wasn't as if they were performing on Broadway where she could become a big star.

Kenneth had no motive that she could tell since he'd already told his wife that he had been gambling again and was in debt. He had to expect that George might quit supporting the theater financially if Celeste wasn't in the play, and he couldn't afford that.

George still bothered her. If she thought the person who had tampered with the balcony had meant to kill Celeste, then George would be her number one suspect. He had a failing business and a one-million-dollar life insurance policy that he would now collect. But if she had been injured, he wouldn't have gained a thing.

Peter was a criminal, it was true, and a liar, but he had no motive to harm Celeste and his feelings for her seemed real. But she'd seen him on stage, and he was a very good actor. Did he act so broken up over her death just to throw off suspicion? Maybe she knew about his past as a jewel thief and threatened to turn him in. But that wouldn't be much of a threat unless she had proof.

"Keiko," Max said, and Keiko looked up from her sewing. "Can you check what the statute of limitations is on jewel theft? I guess it would be grand theft."

"Sure, no problem." Keiko stopped what she was doing and pulled out her laptop.

"I'll be back in a minute." Max went down the hall to Olivia's office.

After entering, she asked Olivia if she had files on the actors with their employment information.

"Kenneth has those files in his office," Olivia said. "They're confidential."

"When is Kenneth going to get here today?" Max asked.

"I'm not participating in anything illegal," Olivia said, giving Max a suspicious look.

"You're such a rule follower," Max said. "I am, too, except when there's a murderer who needs to be caught. I'm not asking you to do anything except tell me when Kenneth is coming in."

"He's supposed to get here around five," Olivia said. "But you're on your own."

"That's fine with me. How about we just agree we didn't have this conversation?"

"What conversation?" Olivia said with a grin.

Max went next door to Kenneth's office and was pleased to find the door wasn't locked. Inside, she found a filing cabinet stuffed with papers. She went through several drawers before she found one with applications stacked in a messy pile. They could really use a file clerk. She paged through the applications until she found Heather's. It wasn't like a regular employment application, just contact information attached to her acting resume, but there was a work number listed. Max took a picture of it with her phone, closed the drawer and slipped out of Kenneth's office.

She walked down the hallway, her heart beating wildly. She didn't know what she would have told Kenneth if she'd been caught. The truth, she supposed.

Max stood in the hall and dialed the number Heather had listed as her work number. She asked for

Heather's manager at the company where she did data entry.

"I'm calling from the Crystal Shores Playhouse where she's currently performing," Max said. She wasn't lying. "We just wanted to confirm the dates she worked there." Max had learned that employers couldn't give out much more information than that.

"Very well. Let me pull up her file." Max waited for more than a minute. "She was employed from May 23rd through June 15th."

"Can you tell me why she left?" It didn't hurt to ask.

"I'm sorry, I can't give out that information," the woman said as Max expected.

"Thank you," Max said and disconnected. June 15th was the day after Celeste died.

CHAPTER 27

Keiko looked up when Max entered. "Four years in California."

"What?" Max asked. Her mind was a jumble of thoughts.

"The statute of limitations for felony theft. Remember, you asked me to look it up?"

"Oh, right. Thanks. He hasn't stolen anything for five years, according to him."

"Do you believe him?" Keiko asked.

"I do. There haven't been any jewel thefts in the area that I know of."

"It would be easy to drive up to L.A."

"True," Max agreed. "But when he told me about taking Celeste's ring, he sounded very much like an addict who hadn't had a fix for a long time. I believe him. And I know he's a very good actor, but I think his grief over Celeste's death is real. He hasn't been himself since she died. It's hard to put on an act 24/7."

Max got back to work on Eric's alterations, since he

would be arriving soon. Luckily, she could sew when her mind was on other things. Something told her she was getting close to solving the murder.

At seven, the actors began to arrive. Max had a plan, but she knew from experience that murderers didn't like it when you figured out they were guilty, so she decided to text Detective Cruz and ask if he could stop by. She sent Keiko to the dressing room to see if any of the women needed help with their costumes.

"Shall I take Heather's blue dress to her?" she asked.

"I just need ten more minutes to finish it," Max said, pretending to sew the hem. "Let her know she can come and get it before the show starts."

It was good to have some quiet time to figure out if she was on the right track or just running down another blind alley. There was only one way to find out, as far as she could tell.

Max heard soft footsteps and teacups rattling on a tray. Looking up, she saw Evelyn standing just inside the door. Max jumped up and grabbed the tray from her, setting it down on the table.

Tea sounded really good right now, but Max didn't want Evelyn in the costume shop at this particular moment.

"Thank you so much, but I really need to be alone to get some work done right now," Max said in her kindest voice.

"Do you plan to have children, my dear?" Evelyn asked in her feeble voice.

"What?" This was not the time for a long conversation about her future plans. "Yes, Evelyn. I want two.

Preferably one of each. Now, I really need to get back to work."

"Oh, of course, dear," Evelyn said, handing her a cup of black tea. "Sugar?"

"I can take care of that myself," Max said.

"I'm sorry. I'm in your way, aren't I?"

"It's not that—" Max started talking just as Detective Cruz entered the room.

"Grandmother?" he said. "What are you doing here?"

"Hello, sweetie. I'm just visiting Max here. She's a lovely girl, just like you said."

Max stared at the detective who shook his head and looked decidedly embarrassed. "How did you get here?"

"I have an app on my phone, dear. Everyone at the senior center uses it. You just tap on the little picture and a nice young person comes and takes you wherever you want to go. I get lonely in my little apartment all by myself. You haven't come to visit for a very long time."

"I took you to dinner on Monday. I've been very busy with work. I'll come to see you on Saturday, I promise."

"That would be lovely. I'd better be on my way now. Max is very busy, too. Young people are so busy nowadays."

Max watched Evelyn shuffle away. Why were grandmothers so good at making you feel guilty?

Detective Cruz saw Evelyn's cookies and said, "May I?" When Max nodded, he took the plate and sat on the sofa with them. “I just happened to mention you to my grandmother once,” he said sheepishly. “I’m sorry if she’s been bothering you.”

“Not at all. She’s awesome.” Max wondered what he had told Evelyn. Apparently, enough to make her curious. Was that why she came to the theater? To check her out? To see if she was good enough for her grandson? The thought made her smile. Then she remembered why she had asked him there. “Thanks for coming. I really appreciate it.”

“What do you have planned, Max? It might help if I knew what you were up to.”

Before Max could answer, Heather arrived at the door. “I need the blue dress. I wear it in the first act. I don’t care if it’s done or not.”

“It’s done,” Max said, but didn’t give it to her. “Mind if we have a little chat?”

“Now? I have to get ready. I’m going on soon.”

“This won’t take long,” Max promised.

“What is this about?” Heather asked nervously, just then noticing the detective sitting on the sofa. Her eyes darted from him back to Max.

“This is about Celeste’s death,” Max said. The detective’s eyebrows rose with curiosity. He hadn’t expected a show, and she was hoping her acting skills were up to the task. “I know you didn’t mean to kill her.”

“What are you talking about?” Heather’s voice went up nearly an octave. “I didn’t do anything.”

“But you really wanted to play Juliet, didn’t you? Celeste was too old. It wasn’t fair that Kenneth gave her the part.”

"No, it wasn't fair. But that doesn't mean I tried to kill Celeste."

"Of course not. She wasn't supposed to die, was she? Just be injured enough that she couldn't do the part and you'd have to step in."

"No, you've got it all wrong. I've got carpel tunnel. I couldn't possibly have loosened the bolts."

"And you were on disability from your last job when they gave you the role of Juliet the day after Celeste died?"

"That's right."

"Except it's wrong." She glanced at Detective Cruz who was hanging on every word, then continued. "You quit your last job the day after Celeste died." She was guessing, but she was pretty sure she was right.

"How do you know that?"

"Never mind. And of all the people there the night we had pizza, you came to me to open your bottle of water. Because you knew I was looking into the murder. I was the one person you wanted to convince that you couldn't have killed Celeste."

"She wasn't supposed to die!" she said suddenly. Wow, it actually worked. "He said she might sprain an ankle or break an arm, but he never said she might die. I never would have done it if I had imagined she'd be dead." She started to sob. "She was horrible to me. She told me I was a terrible actress and I'd never play Juliet."

Max was confused. "Who is 'he'?" She looked up just as Brian came through the door.

Heather closed her mouth and sniffled, wiping her nose with the back of her hand.

"Don't say another word without a lawyer, Heather," Brian told her, and put his arm around her. She leaned on his shoulder and started sobbing.

Detective Cruz stood up. "Heather Lamarque, you're under arrest. You have the right to remain silent…"

When he'd finished reading Heather her rights, Max tried to mouth, "Who's he?"

"You're going to jail," the detective told Heather, "but you'll be charged with manslaughter, so you'll be out before too long. That is, if you tell us who talked you into this. Otherwise, you may be an old lady before you get out of jail."

Max wondered if what he was saying was true or if it was his way of getting her to talk. Heather looked at Cruz and then Max, who nodded.

"Don't say another word, Heather," Brian said, stepping in front of her so she could only see his face. His voice softened as he spoke to her. "They're lying to you. If you don't want to go to jail, don't tell them anything."

"But Brian—" Max began.

"Shut up," he snapped. "Quit badgering her. Can't you see how upset she is? She needs a lawyer."

Max stared at him, at the coldness in his eyes, and the truth came to her in an instant. "This was your idea, wasn't it? You never stopped hating Celeste. She tormented you back in school, and then, when you finally got your dream role and your chance at an

Equity card, she held it over your head that she could get you fired."

"You don't know what you're talking about," Brian said. "You have no proof of any of this."

"I may not have proof, but if you think Heather's going to jail to save your butt, then I'm afraid you're going to be proven wrong."

Detective Cruz handcuffed Heather and Brian and called for backup. Officer Daniels was there fifteen minutes later. Max followed Detective Cruz and Officer Daniels as they led Heather and Brian onto the stage with their hands cuffed behind them.

"What's going on?" Kenneth asked.

"I'm sorry about your play, Kenneth," Detective Cruz said, "but I'm arresting Romeo and Juliet."

CHAPTER 28

Olivia was a magnificent Juliet and only flubbed one line. She had played Juliet in college and after being there for all the rehearsals, she knew the part quite well. Tim, Brian's understudy, was wooden, but serviceable. Max thought once he got over his nerves, he'd probably do a decent job.

The actors and audience gathered in the patio area behind the theater for an opening night reception. Opening night was usually sold out, and tonight was no exception, but the whole run of the show was sold out for four weeks. There was talk of extending the run.

Max got in a long line for champagne. Darlene and Kenneth came up to her to say hello. They looked every bit the loving couple, with Darlene clinging to Kenneth's arm and Kenneth smiling proudly.

The couple pulled Max out of line, and she followed them reluctantly to a quiet corner of the patio. She felt like she really deserved a drink after everything she'd been through for the last eight days, but Darlene insisted.

"Kenneth and I have made a decision," Darlene began, "and I wanted to tell you before you heard it from anyone else." Darlene was positively beaming. Max was happy that Kenneth and Darlene seemed to have patched up their differences.

"What is it?" Max asked.

"I'm retiring," Darlene announced.

"And so am I," Kenneth chimed in. "We're going to travel. We've talked about it for years, but we've both been too busy."

"We're going to sell our house and buy an RV. We'll start by seeing the country and go from there."

"What?" Max didn't know what else to say. She looked from one to the other. They both looked happier than she'd ever seen them. "But what about the shop? And the theater?"

"I was thinking," Darlene said, "since you want to run your own bridal shop, I was wondering if you would consider buying Wedding Belles. After all, it's a great location."

"Are you kidding me?" Max couldn't believe her ears. "That would be amazing!"

Darlene smiled warmly, looking like a woman without a care in the world. "Well, this is a party, so let's wait until Monday to talk business. See when Eric is available, and we'll go over all the details then."

Max looked around for Eric and caught a glimpse of Olivia, surrounded by admirers, not the least of whom was Zach, who looked at her lovingly. "What about the theater?" she asked. She hoped Kenneth didn't plan to shut it down.

"I'll still be on the board, but we'll be hiring a new artistic director. I have someone in mind," Kenneth said, nodding his head in Olivia's direction. "I hope you can keep it to yourself until I have a chance to run it by the board. I'm sure they'll agree she's the ideal person for the job."

Max almost felt like she didn't need a glass of champagne. She was floating on air. Then she remembered how hard she'd been working and got back into line. She bought three glasses of champagne.

Max gave one glass to Keiko but had trouble reaching Olivia to give her the champagne since she was still surrounded by admirers. She noticed that Olivia already had a full glass, so she turned around to see who else she could give it to. She was surprised to see Detective Cruz on the edge of the crowd.

"I'm going to say hi to Detective Cruz," Max told Keiko.

"You go ahead, I'm going to talk to Fiona," Keiko said. Was Keiko leaving them alone on purpose?

She walked up to the detective and handed him the glass, which he accepted.

"Oh good, that means you're off duty." When he agreed, she asked, "Did you see the play?"

"Yes, Kenneth invited me. It was my first Shakespeare play. I'm not sure I understood everything, but I think I actually liked it. The end was really sad."

Max thought he might be the only person in the audience who hadn't known how the play would end.

"Yes, that's why they call it a tragedy," Max teased. "So, Detective Cruz, does this mean we'll be seeing you at the theater more often?"

"If you're going to be here, it just might. And you're supposed to call me Jason, remember?"

"Jason." Max felt awkward calling him by his first name. "That's going to take some getting used to."

"Well, I want you to get used to it."

Max's heart did another flip flop, which was getting to be a habit when he was around. She had to admit he was starting to grow on her. Sure, he was handsome, but he was also considerate and thoughtful. But now that the case was closed, would she even see him again?

"I'll try," she agreed. "But there are some things I'll never get used to, like people I know turning out to be murderers. And to think I was dating him!"

"He didn't mean for her to die," Jason said. "If it makes you feel any better."

"It does and it doesn't. The first date I've had in almost a year, and he turns out to be a manipulative user. I feel like an idiot. I mean, how did I not see through him? I don't think I'm going on another date for quite a while."

"Oh, really." Jason looked at her sympathetically. "How long would that be?"

"I'll let you know." Maybe the next time she saw him? She'd have to run into him one of these days.

"Please do," he said, and raised his glass. "To the future and moving on."

"I'll drink to that," Max said and clinked his glass.

THANK YOU FOR READING MURDER IN CRIMSON VELVET! The next book in the series is Murder in Blue Gingham.

Sign up for Karen's Cozy Club emails at www.karensuewalker.com. Or drop me a line at karen@karensuewalker.com and say hello. I always love to hear from readers like you!

WHAT'S NEXT FOR MAX, KEIKO AND THE REST OF THE GANG?

Read Murder in Blue Gingham and find out!

The only thing worse than an unexpected guest is an unexpected murder!

Max Walters is preparing for her best friend Olivia's wedding when Olivia's childhood friend arrives unannounced. Max joins all the out-of-town friends at a rented beach house for a pre-wedding party where the drinks are flowing, and old grudges seem close to the surface.

When one of the guests is murdered, nearly everyone is a suspect, including Olivia. Can Max clear her name and find the murderer before she becomes the next victim?

Get Murder in Blue Gingham now.

BRIDAL SHOP COZY MYSTERIES

Murder in White Lace
Murder in Crimson Velvet
Murder in Blue Gingham
Murder in Lavender Silk
Murder in Pink Taffeta

Karen Sue Walker also writes the Haunted Tearoom Cozy Mysteries featuring April May who is haunted by the ghost of a French Chef.

Karen also writes humorous action-adventure mysteries as KC Walker. Check out the Arrow Investigations Mysteries!

Printed in Great Britain
by Amazon

28487292R00148